THE TRADING GAME

THE TRADING GAME

Alfred Slote

HarperCollins*Publishers*

Library of Congress Cataloging-in-Publication Data
Slote, Alfred.
  The trading game / by Alfred Slote.
    p.   cm.
  Summary: During a summer of baseball and baseball card trading, eleven-
year-old Andy makes discoveries about his father, his grandfather, who played
professional baseball, and himself.
    ISBN 0-397-32397-2 : $. — ISBN 0-397-32398-0 (lib. bdg.) :
$
  [1. Baseball—Fiction. 2. Baseball cards—Fiction. 3. Fathers
and sons—Fiction. 4. Grandfathers—Fiction.] I. Title.
PZ7.S635Trb 1990   89-12851
[Fic]—dc20   CIP
                                                            AC

In memory of my father, Oscar Slote

THE TRADING GAME

1

It was a Saturday morning in July. Tubby, Kyle Reavy, and I were biking home from another bad baseball practice. The worst part was that our so-called coach, Mr. Cartwright, had scheduled another practice for tomorrow.

Only Tubby was cheerful. One, because he didn't really care about the team. He was only playing because his father was making him. And secondly, 'cause we were going to stop at The Grandstand, where he was going to buy some baseball cards.

"You guys can have the gum," he said.

Kyle looked at me and shook his head. "Tubs is disgusting," he said.

Tubby laughed. Insults flowed off him like water off a duck's back.

The light changed and we shot across the intersection and locked our bikes together around a tree in front of The Grandstand.

3

As we went in, old Mr. Kessler looked at us sourly. Even though he ran a great store for kids, I don't think he really liked kids. He always looked suspicious and the worst things we'd do, horsing around with the stuff, never surprised him.

The fact was, you could do a lot of horsing around in The Grandstand. There were tons of baseball cards, sports magazines, sports books, pennants, caps, newspapers, soft drinks, and candy. It was an old-fashioned store. Dad used to come here when he was a kid.

Once, I complained to Dad about Mr. Kessler being so grumpy all the time. Dad laughed and said: "That's OK, Andy, grumpy storekeepers usually run great stores. It's the smilers you've got to watch out for."

"Why?"

"Because they're not selling anything but themselves. The best thing about The Grandstand, Andy, is the great stuff in there and the fact that old man Kessler leaves you alone with it. You know that standing there in the paperback section I once read *The Joe DiMaggio Story*, the whole book, in two hours and he never bothered me once to buy it? In fact, I didn't think he even noticed me but when I was leaving, he said: 'Pretty good book, huh?' "

4

"Why does he run a store if he doesn't like it and doesn't mind people not buying things?"

"I think he does it to get out of the house," Mom said. "Mrs. Kessler is a battle-axe."

"I'll never marry a battle-axe," I said.

Dad laughed. "They don't start out as battle-axes, Andy. They get that way."

And he ducked as Mom threw a linen napkin across the table at him. In the napkin ring!

Sometimes those memories come back in a rush. Sometimes I'll sit alone in the backyard and try to remember and nothing comes.

Anyway, that Saturday morning in July, Tubby and Kyle and I went into The Grandstand.

"Hi, Mr. Kessler," Tubby said. Tubs was one of Mr. Kessler's best customers. But Mr. Kessler didn't even answer him. He looked at me.

"Your grampa here yet?"

I was really surprised. How'd he know my grampa was coming today?

Tubby was interested right away. "You didn't tell me your grampa was coming to visit you, Andy."

"Why would Andy tell you?" Kyle said, picking out a baseball magazine. "You won't give him *the* card. You're lucky he talks to you at all."

"I won't give it to him but I'll trade with him,"

Tubby said. He gave me a meaningful look. I ignored him.

"He's supposed to be here around noon, Mr. Kessler," I said.

"Tell him to give me a call. I want to chew the fat with him."

"That means they want to eat you, Tubs," Kyle said.

Tubs laughed. That's the trouble with Tubby. He doesn't care about how he looks . . . or plays. Also, I think he may have been a little embarrassed about Kyle mentioning *the* card in front of Mr. Kessler. Mr. Kessler knew he had it, of course.

Kyle and I bought Pepsis while Tubby looked at card sets.

Kyle took a big swallow. "You think your grampa would come to our practice tomorrow?"

"If I asked him." That's what I said but I wasn't so sure. Lots of times, over the phone, I'd asked Grampa to come to my baseball games but he never did.

"Ask him, then," Kyle said. "Things are gettin' desperate. We need help fast."

"You're telling me."

"I'll buy this set, Mr. Kessler," Tubby said.

We watched Tubby give Mr. Kessler forty cents and rip open the pack.

"Here, you guys," he said, giving us the gum while he checked out his cards.

"What'd you get, Tubs?" we asked.

"Don Baylor, who I got four of already. Brett Butler, who I got two of. Mark Clear, who'll be worth two cents even after his career. Jim Fregosi, manager . . . I got him too. LaMarr Hoyt. He could be worth something someday."

"You know what, Tubs?" Kyle said.

"What?"

"You think about money too much."

"What else is there to think about? Here's Joaquin Andujar . . . traded from the Cards. Marc Sullivan. His father is one of the owners of the Red Sox. Hmmm . . . they might come out with a father-son series, only the father's an owner and the son's a player."

Kyle and I laughed. We chewed Tubby's gum. It would have been better chewing the cards.

Tubby also got a Ruppert Jones he didn't need, a Rick Burleson he didn't want. And then he chortled triumphantly.

"How about this?"

"What?" we both said, looking.

"Wally Joyner, rookie all-star card. I bet that's worth some money."

Tubby grabbed the dog-eared price guide that was chained to the counter.

"Hey, you guys, it's worth $2.25. How about that? I more than quadrupled my money already. And these other cards are probably worth another dollar for all of them. Mr. Kessler, can I have a plastic sleeve?"

Mr. Kessler, without looking at him, shoved a cigar box of plastic sleeves across the counter. Mr. Kessler was keeping a suspicious eye on some third-graders looking at Tigers T-shirts.

"Have to protect my investment, you know," Tubby said.

"You know something, Tubs?" Kyle said. "You got dollar signs in your eyes."

"That's why you can't hit or catch," I said.

He laughed. "The only reason I can't hit or catch, Andy, is 'cause I'm terrible. If my dad didn't sponsor our team I wouldn't have to play at all. Which would be all right with me because then I could work on my baseball card show."

"What baseball-card show?" we asked, surprised.

"I'm gonna have a big baseball-card show in my backyard this summer. My dad said it was OK. He's gonna have one of his carpenters make up a sign to put on my tree house. *Swap 'n' Sell.* Pretty catchy, huh?"

I thought it *was* pretty catchy. I could picture it nailed to Tubby's tree house. And kids all milling around below swapping and selling and Tubby directing operations from above.

Kyle, grinning, shook his head. "I think you ought to call it The Watson Baseball Card Company and be done with it."

I laughed. I knew what Kyle meant. Just about everywhere you went in Arborville you saw the name "Watson" on a business. Tubby's dad owned a car dealership, a dry cleaners, a laundry, an ice-cream factory, and a lot of apartment houses. The name of our team was Watson Chevrolet. But it could have been The Watson Dry Cleaning Company, The Watson Laundry Company, the Watson Ice-Cream Company, or The Watson Real Estate Company.

"I thought about that," Tubby said, taking Kyle seriously. "But that's gonna be the name of the store I open someday. That or Tree House Baseball Cards."

Tubby did all his serious trading in his tree house.

"You know what I'm gonna do with this Wally Joyner card?" Tubby said.

"Frame it," Kyle said.

"Nope. I'm gonna use it to swap Cartwright for one of her two '68 Al Kalines. I don't have him for that year. She's coming to the tree house this afternoon."

Kyle gave me a nudge. "Tubs and Alice Cartwright trading cards in his tree house."

For once, something got to Tubby. His face turned red and he began to splutter.

"She's got some great cards, Kyle. And who knows what kind of career Joyner will have? She's got a whole set of the St. Louis Cardinals Gas House Gang, two 1937 Pepper Martins, and Ducky Medwick, who I don't have."

"You're makin' these names up," Kyle said.

"Hey, Mr. Kessler, am I making up Ducky Medwick and Pepper Martin?"

"No," Mr. Kessler said, unsurprised at being appealed to. There were always a lot of baseball arguments in The Grandstand, and Mr. Kessler was always the ump.

"See?" Tubby beamed. He had succeeded in changing the subject back to baseball cards and away from him and Alice Cartwright in his tree house. Alice was our third baseman. She was tough as nails, a tomboy, and a better ball player than most of the guys on the team.

"Mr. Kessler, do you have an Olympic Mark McGwire?" Tubby asked.

"No," Mr. Kessler grunted. "No" was his favorite word.

"I'm gonna start collecting Mark McGwires. You know why?" Tubby said to us.

"'Cause he was American League Rookie of the Year in '87," I said.

"Nope," Tubby said. "'Cause of his batting stance. I figured out a new specialty card for Aces. I'm gonna write them about it. Strange-batting-stance cards. Like McGwire with his left foot turned in, Stan Musial in a corkscrew, Mel Ott lifting his right leg. Al Simmons' foot in the bucket. I bet you guys don't know who Al Simmons is, do you?"

"No, and we don't want to know," Kyle said.

"Tubs, if there's an Olympic Mark McGwire card in my dad's collection, would you trade for that?"

Tubby's eyes turned crafty. "There's a lot of those Olympic team sets around, Andy. One'll turn up here. But there's only one *Ace 459 Jim Harris 1b*, as far as I know. Your grampa just didn't play long enough."

Kyle finished his Pepsi and put the bottle in the empties case. "You know something, Tubs? You're a real louse."

"Aw, Kyle, baseball cards are *my* game. I don't see you giving anything away when you run the bases."

Kyle, who was the fastest kid in the Arborville eleven-year-old baseball league, didn't know what to say to that. He didn't know how anyone could think playing ball and collecting baseball cards were equal things.

Tubby laughed. "Here, Kyle, I'll give you a Don Baylor and you can have the Rick Burleson, Andy."

"No thanks," I said.

"I'll take 'em both," Kyle said.

"You collecting cards now, Reavy?" I asked.

"In my spokes," Kyle said, grinning.

Tubby made a face. He was sorry now he'd given him the cards. We went outside and watched Kyle unlock his bike and put Don Baylor between the front spokes and Rick Burleson in the rear wheel. Tubs shook his head disapprovingly.

"See you chumps tomorrow," Kyle said, and took off up Arch Street. We could hear Don Baylor and Rick Burleson going *flipityflipflipflip* all the way up the street.

"Kyle's gonna be poor all his life," Tubby said.

"So what?"

"It's dumb to be poor when you don't have to be." Tubs looked at me. "You see Mr. Kessler give me the plastic sleeves for nothing?"

"Yeah."

"He does that 'cause my family's rich. Rich people always get stuff for nothing."

"So what? I'd rather run and hit like Kyle

12

than be rich and strike out like you. Let's go."

We started pedaling up Packard in the bike lane. Tubby rode on the inside . . . protecting his investment.

"Is your grampa bringing your dad's card collection with him?" Tubby asked me around the intersection of Packard and East U.

"If Helen sent it to him, he will."

"She's supposed to, isn't she?"

"I don't know about supposed to. She said she would. But she could change her mind."

"I hope she doesn't," Tubby said. He was beginning to puff hard. "If you (*puff*) get your dad's cards (*puff*) you and I could do some trading." *Puff, puff, puff.*

I slowed down. Don't look too eager, I told myself. Tubs may look like a whale on the ball field but he was a shark around baseball cards.

"Can I meet your grampa when he comes?" Tubby asked.

"Maybe," I grunted, and pedaled away from him.

Tubby pedaled harder to keep up. "My grampa said he saw your grandfather play at Tiger Stadium, only it was called Briggs Stadium then. That's where Ace took your grandfather's picture."

He's working on me, I thought. Reminding

me again about *the* card. He didn't have to. I wanted that card more than anything else on earth.

Tubby had the only card I'd ever seen of Grampa. It showed him at first base reaching for a throw. *Ace 459 Jim Harris 1b*, it said on the front.

On the back it had Grampa's stats for his three years with Beaumont (Texas League, Class A) before the war and his one year with the Tigers in 1945. Grampa jumped from Class A to the major leagues. He'd been discharged early from the Army because of a shell fragment in his left forearm. It didn't hurt him any playing ball.

In 1945, the year of the card, he hit .278 for the Tigers and the Tigers won the American League pennant. Grampa didn't get to play in the World Series because late in the season Hank Greenberg returned from the war and took his position back.

The next spring Grampa was traded to Cleveland. He hurt his back in a pregame pepper practice in Florida and never did play much again. He had an operation after the season but it wasn't a success. And the year after that, Grampa took a job teaching school in Arborville, where Dad was born and where I was born too.

When Grampa retired, he and Grandma

moved to Arcadia, Michigan, near Frankfurt on the big lake. Grandma died about five years ago and Grampa lives alone now. He doesn't have much money but he can do a lot of fishing.

Anyway, about Grampa's card. Tubby had found it in a store in Livonia. I offered to buy it from him but he wouldn't sell.

I got Dad to take me to that store but we couldn't find another one. In *The Baseball Card Digest* its value was twenty-five cents, which means it wasn't valuable.

It was a lot more valuable to me. Mr. Kessler said he would keep an eye out for another one, but that was a while ago and it hasn't turned up yet.

I asked Dad once why he didn't trade Tubby for it.

Dad smiled. "I think Tubby should have it. He's building a great collection."

"Wouldn't you like to have your father's card?"

Dad smiled.

"You could advertise for it, then."

Dad laughed. "Advertise for a twenty-five-cent card?"

I remember Mom giving me a look that said: "Get off the subject, Andy."

I didn't understand that look then.

Anyway, I offered Tubs all the money I had

in the world—twenty-two dollars in piggy banks—for the card, but Tubs refused.

"It's a one-of-a-kind, Andy," he said to me.

Which meant he wanted more money. I guessed one day Tubby would be a big business-man in Arborville like his father and grand-father.

Looking back on it, I guess the mistake was Dad showing Tubby his collection. You couldn't miss the gleam in Tubby's eyes as Dad showed him his cards.

Dad had a 1952 Mickey Mantle worth $2500. Not to mention a 1952 Willie Mays and a 1939 rookie Ted Williams.

I *know* Tubs has his eye on Dad's collection. And I have my eye on *the* card. It looked like it would be a battle royal between us.

I stood up on my bike and started pedaling hard. Tubby shouted to wait up. He wanted to talk more about cards.

"Not interested," I lied, and left him behind in the dust.

2

Grampa's old Buick was not there. That was the first thing I looked for as I biked over the Granger-Ferdon intersection and into the lane where we lived.

What was there, the first thing I saw, was Mom kneeling in front of the garden bed.

I shot over the curb and squeezed my brakes hard, skidding to a stop six inches from her back.

"Is it Mario Andretti?" Mom asked without turning around.

"Mario Junior," I said.

"Is there a Mario Junior?" She pulled out a big weed.

"Sure. Only his name is Michael. Don't you know anything about sports?"

"Knowing fathers and sons isn't knowing about sports."

"Yes it is. They've got father-and-son baseball cards. Tubby has a whole bunch: Roy Smalley Sr. and Roy Smalley Jr., Tito and Terry Francona, Ray and Bob Boone, Jim and Mike Hegan, Bob and Terry Kennedy, Ken Griffey and Ken—"

"Enough," Mom said. "I concede." She turned around and looked up at me, pulling a strand of hair away from her eyes. She was sweating. She had worked up more of a sweat pulling weeds than we had playing baseball.

"Aren't you back early?"

"Only six kids showed up for practice."

"How come?"

"Mr. Cartwright is a lousy coach. That's how come." I laid my bike down in the grass. "We'll be lucky if we get nine people to show up Monday for our first game."

"Who was there?" Mom asked, going back to weeding.

"Alice Cartwright, of course. The Gomez twins and me, Reavy, and Tubby Watson. The only reason Tubby comes is because of his father. Mom, we're going to bomb again this season. We're playing the Warren Plumbers on Monday. They finished first last year. We'd give them a closer game by not showing up."

"Well," Mom said, dropping an enormous weed in the basket, "you better do something about it, then."

"You don't understand. We can't do anything as long as Mr. Cartwright's coaching us." I squatted down beside her. "You think Grampa might coach us while he's here?"

"No," Mom said promptly.

"He's never coached me on a team. He's never even seen me play in a game."

"He knows you're good, Andy."

"But what about the team? It'd be good for the team. We're falling apart right now."

"Please don't ask him to coach, Andy."

"Why not? What's he going to do here all summer? He'll be bored silly."

"Grampa's not going to spend the whole summer with us."

"You said he might."

"I said he might *have* to if his tests were bad. And then he probably won't be in any shape to coach anyone."

"What's wrong with Grampa, anyway?"

Mom hesitated. "He's sixty-five. When your body gets to be sixty-five it feels pains."

"Connie Mack coached when he was over eighty."

"Who's he?" She went on weeding.

"You're kidding. He was only one of the original Hall of Famers. He managed the Philadelphia A's in the twenties and thirties. Dad's got three Connie Mack cards. Listen, Tubby was talking to me about Dad's cards. Can I—"

"No," Mom said, knowing what I was going

to ask. "You're not going to call Grampa again. Besides, he left Arcadia hours ago."

"You think he remembered to bring Dad's cards?"

"If he has them, he remembered. Your grandfather doesn't forget things."

"She promised to send them to him."

"Well, let's hope she did." Mom dropped a dandelion root in the basket. "How about emptying this for me?"

"OK."

I emptied the basket in the green barrel by our garage. By the time I got back, Mom had a whole bunch more weeds on the walk. She was an attack gardener. The Pete Rose of gardening.

I put the new weeds into the basket.

"Suppose Grampa is OK, Mom, and the doctor says he can do anything he wants. Including coaching. What would be wrong with me asking him to coach us? He's an ex–major leaguer. He coached high school baseball."

Mom sighed. "You have a one-track mind, you know that?"

"Well, what would be wrong?"

Mom shifted position as she went after another dandelion. "All right, one thing that would be wrong is that it would be very rude to Mr.

Cartwright. He volunteered to coach you when no one else would. You wouldn't have a team at all if it wasn't for him."

"We don't have a team with him. Besides, he didn't volunteer."

Mom looked surprised. "What do you mean?"

"The reason he's coaching is because Mr. Watson's making him."

"That's nonsense."

"It's not nonsense. Mr. Cartwright's law firm does a lot of work for Tubby's family. All those Watson companies. Tubby's dad told Mr. Cartwright that Watson Chevrolet needed a coach and since Mr. Cartwright also had a kid on the team, he better coach."

"I don't believe that for a second."

"Ask Tubby. He told me that himself. Tubby's dad is tough. You know something, if I told Mr. Watson that Grampa was willing to coach us, he'd fire Mr. Cartwright, bango. Just like that."

"Please don't tell him, then. And please don't ask Grampa to coach or even help coach."

"Mom, you act as though Grampa's above coaching kids' baseball. He coached Dad's Little League team when Dad was a kid."

"Yes, he did, and it didn't work out."

"What happened, anyway?" It was a subject Dad would never talk about. Nor would Grampa.

Nor, I guess, would Mom. "Would you move the basket a little closer to me?" was her answer now.

"Things are really great," I said sarcastically. "No one will tell me what happened when Grampa coached Dad. And I'm not supposed to ask Grampa to coach me. And I can't call him up and remind him to bring the cards."

Mom looked up at me. "You're being a real pest, Andy. Go ahead and call him. I told you he won't be there. And he's already told you at least four different times that if Helen sends him the cards he'll bring them."

"I guess she's the one I should've called."

"You wouldn't have got her either."

"Why not?"

Using her two-pronged green dandelion tool, Mom went down deep, viciously, into the earth.

"Because she and her daughters are on their way to California right now. Furthermore, Andy, she doesn't have to give you a single baseball card. And if she realizes the value of your father's collection, she probably won't."

"But Dad said—"

She pulled out a dandelion root at least a foot long.

"*You* say Dad said, but you don't have it in writing. And we both know how much that lady likes money."

22

Mom bit her lip. She looked at me. "Andy, I don't like talking like this. I'm sure Helen has sent Daddy's cards to Grampa, and if it makes you feel better to call him again, go ahead and do it."

"He won't be there," I said.

She looked startled. And then she laughed. "Get out of here."

"But I'll call anyway," I said, and ran before she could throw the foot-long dandelion root at me.

There was no answer in Grampa's house. I could picture the phone ringing on the round table in his kitchen.

Grampa had a little white house about a block from Lake Michigan. He was two blocks from the marina, where he had a little outboard. He and I would go fishing on the big lake when it wasn't rough. The big lake is what folks around Arcadia call Lake Michigan.

I would rather play baseball with him than fish, but Grampa said his baseball days were over.

But one weekend last August the big lake was too rough every day and I finally talked Grampa into playing ball with me.

There's a bumpy ball diamond across U.S. 31 that had been the old high school diamond before they started bussing to the high school in Onekema.

It was on that bumpy diamond that Grampa and I played for the first time.

He looked so tall and easy with his old first baseman's glove. He even looked younger.

We started by throwing easy. "Loosening up the flippers" was how Grampa put it.

Grampa couldn't throw hard anymore. He threw with a sidearm that he said was easy on his arthritis. But you could see the way he caught and threw, the smoothness of it, that he was an old ball player.

We moved apart gradually till it was a sixty-foot throw and then we played catch, till all of a sudden, without warning, Grampa tossed a grounder to me. At first the grounders were right at me but then he started moving me around, to the right, to the left, faking in one direction, throwing in another.

"Play the ball, Andy, don't let it play you."

"You can get in front of those. Move. Don't get lazy on me."

"First you catch it, then you throw it. It's a darn simple game when you get down to it."

"Aim at my head and it'll come in chest high."

"Come over your head when you throw. When you get old like me, you can throw sidearm."

Only once did he actually compliment me. I

25

scooped up a shorthopper and winged it back at him in one motion.

He smiled and said. "You look natural, Andy."

That's all he said, but it was a lot.

After that, Grampa picked up a bat and started hitting those same ground balls to me, 'cause he said batted balls have different spins and take different bounces than thrown balls. And a batted ball off a pitch is *still* different.

Grampa was an artist with the bat. He hit little pop-ups moving me this way, and then in and out. When I threw back to him, he'd catch it with his bare left hand and in a sweeping motion he'd put another ball just where he wanted it.

We had a little pepper practice. I'd throw and he'd hit and he could do the same thing with the ball. Hit it to a spot the size of a dime.

Then he surprised me. He went to his old Buick and out of the trunk he brought a bag of baseballs.

"Where'd you get those?" I asked.

He laughed. "You never know when you'll need a baseball on the road."

He emptied them out and then he gave me batting practice. He threw and I hit. And he talked to me.

"Hittin's natural, Andy. Just make yourself comfortable."

"Get your bat back. You don't want to waste time bringin' it back and then up."

"Watch the ball in my hand, watch it leave my hand, and when it gets in over the plate, why, just bring your bat around and hit it. It's a simple game, ain't it, son?"

Grampa made me look good. I hit line drives all over that bumpy old field in Arcadia. Afterward we drove back to his little house.

"I wish you could come coach us in Arborville," I said.

He smiled. "My coachin' days are over."

"No, they're not," I said.

He laughed.

And that was when I asked Grampa what it was like when he coached Dad.

Grampa was silent at first. Then he said, "It was a long time ago, Andy. All I can remember now is that he didn't have the talent you have."

"But what was it like?"

"I said I don't remember." Grampa's voice got hard and I knew enough to drop it.

Funny how those memories keep coming at you.

"What are you doing, Andy?" Mom said.

She'd come in the kitchen, dandelion tool in hand, all dirty and sweaty, and was watching me on the phone.

27

"Waiting for Grampa to answer the phone."

"How many times did it ring?"

"I stopped counting after thirty."

"Andy, I want to speak to you about something."

"What?"

"I want the house quiet when Grampa comes. He's coming two days early to get ready for those tests. I don't want any of your friends over. All right?"

"Tubby's gonna want to come over and look at Dad's cards if Grampa has them."

"That's out."

"OK."

The trading with Tubby would have to be done in his tree house. Which suited me. I liked going into it.

I threw my baseball stuff on the closet floor, went into the bathroom, and turned on the shower. When I got the temperature just right, I stepped in.

That was pretty funny, being caught by Mom waiting for Grampa to answer a phone. Grampa was probably coming into town right now on U.S. 23, shooting straight as a marble for our house.

Grampa drove an old blue Buick that he never washed. When Dad got promoted to head of the Arborville office for his company, he bought

Grampa a one-year-old BMW but Grampa wouldn't take it.

"Nobody'd know me drivin' that, Jamey."

"Come on, Dad," Dad said. "You can take a present from me."

"Not anything that expensive, Jamey."

It made me uneasy to listen to them. Dad was always trying to give Grampa presents, and Grampa was never taking them. Even though he didn't have a lot of money. A little pension from the school system, Social Security, and that was about that.

Once I asked Mom why Grampa wouldn't take things from Dad.

"Pride," Mom said.

"It's no good, then, pride."

"Not when it interferes with love."

"Didn't Grampa love Dad?"

"A lot. But he wasn't able to show it. Grampa couldn't accept things from Dad. It would mean showing love. For some people it's easier to give than it is to receive."

Not for Tubby, I thought. But I guess it was true for Grampa 'cause he was always shaking off Dad.

"Hold on to your money, Jamey," he'd say, waving a big hand at Dad. "I'm doin' fine."

Dad was James Harris, Jr. Dad told me that for a while he was known as Little Jim and

Grampa was Big Jim. "But about when I was seven years old," Dad said, "Grandma started calling me Jamey. She knew long before Grampa that I wasn't ever going to be a ball player. She knew Little Jim would never grow up to be Big Jim."

Old as he was, Grampa was still big. In his ball playing days, and it said so on the back of *the* card, he was six-three and weighed 215 pounds.

Now Grampa said he'd shrunk to six-one and weighed about 170 pounds on a cool day. Dad was a little under six feet. Mom's real short so I probably won't even be as tall as Dad was.

In every other family in the world the kids keep getting bigger than the parents. We're the only family that gets shorter. My children will probably be midgets. If I get married, which I sincerely doubt.

I was eight years old when my mom and dad divorced. Looking back on it now, I guess I should've seen it coming. I guess in a way I did but didn't want to admit it.

Dad was a stockbroker. He was good at it too. Here in Arborville he helped them set up the computer system and got promoted to head of the office. After a while he got promoted to the Detroit office and then to head of that office, and he got offers from other firms and made lots of trips to New York.

One day Dad came home early from Detroit or New York or wherever he was working. Mom was still at school. She teaches English at Arborville High.

Anyway, Dad was waiting for me after school.

"What're you doing here?" I said.

"I came home to talk with you."

Right away I sensed something bad.

"I'm playing ball this afternoon, Dad."

"You can be a little late. How about going over to my old tree house?"

"No." Any other time, I would have. It was a neat place. Dad had built it when he was a kid. And we had rediscovered it together last summer. Which I'll tell you about later.

"We can talk here, then," Dad said.

"The guys are waiting for me at the park, Dad."

That was not exactly true. You went to the park and got into a game. No one ever waited for you to come.

"Sit down, Andy," he said.

I sat down. I had to. I wished I was a million miles away. I knew what was coming. I'd heard Mom cry once after a long-distance phone call from Dad in New York. Then I heard her calling Grandpa and Grandma Marshall, her parents, who live in North Carolina. And then she talked with Grandma and Grampa Harris. (Grandma was alive then.)

You got to be real thick not to know when something bad is happening around you. Half the kids at Sampson Park School's folks are divorced.

So Dad told me what I already knew. That he and Mom thought it was best for them to separate for a while. There was a lot of tension in the house. It would be good for me too if that tension disappeared.

You know how it goes. You've seen it on TV soap operas, or in those goopy made-for-TV movies.

Parents are always getting divorced for their kids' sakes. What bunk.

When Dad got done, all I said was: "I didn't know you and Mom were unhappy."

"We're not," Dad said.

"Then why're you divorcing?"

He just looked at me. I was all of eight years old at the time. It seemed like a simple question, but suddenly he got tears in his eyes and said: "We're not happy, Andy."

"Why not?" I said.

And he stammered around and later it came out that he had fallen in love with a woman named Helen who managed the stockbroker office in Detroit. And now they were both going to move to New Jersey. And on and on he went about this Helen and how I would get to know her and like her and she had two girls my age.

Well, I've met the famous Helen. And I don't like her or her daughters. And they don't like me. And I don't blame them.

I used to go there for Christmas holidays or Thanksgiving, and there was no one to play with in that family. Dad wasn't even there most of the time.

When he got back from New York City at the end of the day (they lived in a big house near a town called Kendall Park, New Jersey), he and I would take a walk or he'd dig out his old green Thom McAn shoe box that contained his baseball cards and we'd go over them. That part was all right.

Dad knew the stats on every ball player who ever lived. He didn't have a big collection. He had traded and sold through the years, and at the end he had only about nine hundred cards including duplicates. Nowhere near as big as Tubby's collection, but there were a lot of quality cards. Like the Mantle one I mentioned earlier.

Dad had made up a computer list of his collection with the value of each card next to the player's name and extra prices where he had duplicates.

For example, for his 1962 set (Dad had collected almost every player in 1962—he was eleven years old that year—my age now in 1989). . . for that 1962 set he had three columns on his computer printout.

The first column had what the card was worth. (According to *The Baseball Card Digest.*)

Let's say it was a 1962 Nellie Fox card. Worth seventy cents. The next column would have the number of cards he had of Nellie Fox. Dad had five Nellie Foxes . . . so number 5 would be there next to Nellie Fox. And finally the last column would have $2.80, which is four times $.70. And the reason it's four times seventy and not five is 'cause Dad was going to keep one card for himself. He'd be willing to trade the other four Nellie Foxes.

So here's the way the Nellie Fox entry would look:

$.70   5 Nellie Fox $2.80

If you added up all the figures in the last column, which Dad did, that became the trading value of his collection.

That 1962 set also included Roger Maris with his great 1961 stats. That was the year he hit 61 homers to break Babe Ruth's record, asterisk or no asterisk. Worth $230 according to *The Baseball Card Digest.*

Dad also had a 1952 Yogi Berra worth fifty-five bucks.

A 1952 Willie Mays worth $450.

And, of course, the great Mantle card.

About a month before the accident, Dad told me over the phone he was trying to trade for one of the most expensive baseball cards around, a 1910 Honus Wagner. This one was worth ten thousand dollars.

A guy in Ohio had it and wanted to sell it. Dad was trying to talk him into a trade. He told me he had put together a package of his best cards and all together they were worth that much but the guy was holding out for cash.

"I may give it to him too." Dad laughed over the phone. "I'd like to own that old Dutchman for a while. To my way of thinking he was the greatest ball player who ever lived."

"Better than Willie Mays?"

"Maybe a teench better than Mays because he did it all from a tough position, shortstop. But they were the same kind of ball player, guys who could do it all. Run, hit, hit for power, field, throw. Honus Wagner was a great shortstop. And toward the end of his career, a great third baseman. A great everything. A legend. I want his card."

Dad used to trade a lot when he was younger. All his cards were in excellent to mint condition.

He kept them in plastic sleeves. Grampa said Dad did that from the time he first started buying bubble-gum cards when he was about six years old.

"Your dad was always a careful little fella," Grampa said. "He always knew the value of a nickel."

Grampa used to say that with scorn in his voice, but I didn't see what was wrong with it. Mom said Grampa meant that kids shouldn't know too early the value of a nickel. Like Tubby? Dad and Tubby? No, Tubs was a joke. Dad wasn't.

Anyway, last Christmas Dad and I figured out that his collection was worth over twenty thousand dollars. And what I say next is the absolute truth, though no one was there to witness it and I don't have a tape of it.

It was snowing out and he and I were holed up in his study in New Jersey going over his cards. Him remembering what he'd paid or who he'd traded for each card. And then he looked at me over the desk light and smiled funny. "You know, Andy, one of these days this collection is going to be yours. Kim and Karen [Helen's daughters] don't care for baseball cards."

I don't have it in writing. Not on tape. No witnesses. I told Grampa later what Dad had said and I told Mom, but I've got no proof.

I didn't think proof would ever be necessary because I didn't think I'd get those cards till I was grown up and maybe he'd just give them to me. But then . . . just two months after he said that to me—it was almost like some deep part of him knew something bad was going to happen to him—we got a phone call from Grampa in Arcadia.

I was home alone when the phone rang. Mom wasn't back from school yet. Grampa didn't have a lot of money. He never called in the middle of the day, when the rates are highest.

"Hi, Grampa. How are you?"

"I'm fine, Andy. Is your mom there?"

"No, she's at work."

His voice sounded funny. Shaky. It could be a bad connection.

"I don't have her number at school, Andy."

"Wait a second. Here." Mom had the high school office number taped on the wall over the upstairs and downstairs phones.

"555–6575. How's the big lake?"

"Rough. How's school?"

"Rough too."

He laughed. It was a scratchy laugh too. "You do good there, boy. School's important."

"You sound like Dad."

He didn't say anything for a second and then he said, "Andy, I'll talk to you later."

And hung up fast. Fast for Grampa. He and I usually noodled on the phone a bit talking sports or about the Tigers. But not today. Well, it was probably 'cause he was calling at an expensive time. Grampa has to watch his pennies.

Anyway, it suited me not to talk too much either because I was on my way over to the park to play shinny. Shinny is fun hockey on the iced-over tennis courts at Sampson Park. Half the time you don't know who you're checking.

I changed into hockey clothes. Then I went downstairs to the hall closet and got out my helmet, mouth guard, pads, gloves, stick, skates. I was halfway out the door when Mom drove into our driveway.

She popped out of the car. "Come back inside, Andy."

"I'm going to the park."

"You can go in a minute. I want to talk to you."

It kicked off a memory. Dad coming home early from work that time to tell me . . .

Mom's scarf fell off. I picked it up. "What's going on? Is Grampa OK? He sounded funny."

She opened the door and I went back in after her.

"Grampa's OK. Please sit down."

Her face was pale. My heart began to pound. It was the whole thing with Dad all over again. We sat there on two chairs facing each other and suddenly I knew it was about Dad. Something had happened to Dad.

Mom started crying. I knew Dad was dead.

I knew it in my skin, in my bones. I knew it without saying the word. And what good does it do to say the word? The word is just another four-letter word.

Mom nips off "dead" flowers in summer; we had a dog and a cat die. Two pet turtles once died the same night.

Besides, I thought, she's mad at him. What's she crying for?

"What happened?" I said.

She wiped her eyes. She told me that Dad had been driving home from New York City last night on the Jersey Turnpike. There was fog. A big semi crashed into a car behind him and caused a chain collision. Six people were killed. Dad was one. Helen had called Grampa this afternoon. She wouldn't call us. She asked him to do that, Mom said bitterly.

Enough with memories.

I turned off the hot water and turned up the cold. Grampa once told me you should always end a hot shower with a cold one. "It closes your pores," he said. Though why it was good to have your pores close, he didn't say.

After the cold shower I wiped the excess water off me with my hands. That was something else Grampa taught me.

"You save on towels that way," he said.

Grampa knew lots of little things like that. Locker-room knowledge.

If he could coach us . . . No, don't think about it. Take things one step at a time. It was enough he was coming. Enough he might be bringing Dad's card collection.

If he had them, then Tubby and I could trade. And I'd see what he wanted for *Ace 459 Jim Harris 1b*. Book value: twenty-five cents.

Suppose he only would trade for the 1952 Mickey Mantle, value $2500. Would I really trade a $2500 card for a twenty-five-cent one?

I got goose pimples just thinking about it.

Well, the answer to goose pimples is dry yourself and get moving. Which I did. I got out of the shower and was drying myself when a car horn sounded outside.

It had to be Ace 459 himself. I took off down the stairs, holding the towel around my hips.

Grampa's tall. He walks tall. Slow, erect, and tall. He has a broken nose and ball hawk-blue eyes. They can look right through you. Which is OK as long as you got nothing to hide.

I grinned. I didn't have anything to hide. All I had around me was a towel.

Grampa smiled. "Looks like you growed about an inch and put on ten pounds."

"I'll take five pounds off his hide if he doesn't get inside the house right away," Mom said. "Mrs. O'Dell is getting an eyeful."

Mrs. O'Dell is a widow lady who lives across the lane from us and spends most of the day looking out her window. She was at the window right now looking at us.

Grampa waved at her. "Emily always was a nosey Parker," he said.

Mrs. O'Dell waved back.

Mom was at the Buick opening the back door.

"What are you doin', Miss?" Grampa said, going to the car.

"Getting your suitcase."

"You put that down. I'm not helpless yet."

"No one's suggesting you are."

As Mom pulled the suitcase out of the car, Grampa made a grab for it. Mom swung it out of his reach and, laughing, went into the house.

"Time was," Grampa said, closing the door, "a woman knew her place."

"We got a girl playing third for us, Grampa," I said. I ran to the front door to hold it open for him.

"She any good?"

He didn't mind my holding the door for him 'cause I was a guy.

"She's OK. But her father's terrible. He's our coach."

He gave me a sharp look. "Don't ever like to hear a player knock a coach, Andy."

"I'm not knocking him, Grampa. I'm just telling the truth. Besides, you'd knock Mr. Cartwright too. He never even played high school ball."

Grampa stood there looking at our living room as if remembering how it used to look. (It looked the same. He just hadn't visited us in a while.)

There was a picture of me, Mom, and Dad

on the mantelpiece. Mom had taken down the pictures of just her and Dad but not the ones that included me. I liked that.

Grampa looked at that picture. "Some of the best managers I had couldn't play worth diddly themselves," he said, still looking at the picture.

"But Grampa, Mr. Cartwright doesn't *know* anything either. We were 1 and 9 last year. And this year we'll be 0 and 10. You know how many kids showed up at our practice this morning?"

We could hear Mom moving around upstairs. "How many?" he asked, looking at me.

"Six. And our first game's Monday. He's scheduled another practice for tomorrow. No one'll come to that either. Grampa, do you—"

Despite my promise not to ask him to coach, the question was about to pop out of my mouth. I think Mom had ESP at that moment because she came down the stairs real fast.

"Andrew Harris, do you intend to spend the rest of the day naked?"

"No."

"Then get upstairs and get dressed."

"OK." I started up the stairs and then I remembered something I *could* ask Grampa. I stopped halfway up and looked down at them. They both looked at me.

"Now what?" Mom said.

"Well, I was just . . . uh . . . wondering if . . . uh . . . Grampa had any more stuff in his car."

I was thinking about a green box that had Thom McAn Shoes on the cover.

Grampa frowned. "There's nothin' else in the car, boy. Your mom got it all."

My face fell.

"Were you lookin' for somethin' particular?" he asked.

"No," I said, and continued on up the stairs.

Grampa laughed and called after me: "You get some clothes on and then you can check out your dad's cards."

I whizzed back down. "You got 'em, Grampa!"

"Yep."

I ran into my room and started getting dressed. The phone rang.

"I'll get it," I shouted. The hall phone was right outside my door.

"Hello?"

"Andy, it's me, Tubby."

"Tubby who?"

"Cut it out, Andy. Is he—"

"Yep. He's here."

"All *right*." Tubby paused. "Did he uh . . ."

"Yep."

"I'm coming over."

44

I remembered Mom's order. "No, you're not."
But then, I didn't want to hurt Tubby's feelings.
So I added, "First *I'm* gonna look at 'em."

"I'll help you."

"I don't need any help."

"Yes, you do," Tubby said, and hung up.

Darn him, I thought. Who did he think he
was? How was I gonna explain this to Mom?

When I got back downstairs, Mom and
Grampa were seated at the dining-room table
drinking tea. Their faces were serious. I guessed
they were talking about Grampa's health. He
looked fine to me.

"Who was that, Andy?" Mom asked.

"Tubby. He wants to come over and see Dad's
cards. I told him no but he's coming anyway. I
won't let him in, Mom. Where are they,
Grampa?"

"In my suitcase. What's wrong with your
friend? He got something catchin'?"

"It's not that, Jim," Mom said. "Andy has the
world's noisiest friends. I think you ought to
rest after your trip."

"Hogwash to that. I like bein' around kids."

I bet he *would* come to our practice and coach
us, I thought.

"Sorry, Jim, but this is my ballpark," Mom
said firmly. "I set the ground rules here."

Grampa winked at me. "You got one tough mom, Andy."

"I know. Where's your suitcase?"

"Where'd you put it, Miss?"

"Up on your bed." Mom hesitated. "You're staying in Jamey's study. I hope it's all right with you. It has the best mattress."

Grampa's face didn't change expression. "That'll be just fine."

"Should I bring your suitcase down, Grampa?"

"No. You go 'head and open it upstairs. The cards are in there, just like she mailed 'em."

"Didn't you look at them?"

"Why would I do that? They were bein' sent for you."

"She might've kept out some of the good ones."

"Andy!" Mom said.

Grampa laughed. "Knowin' her, that's not bad figurin'. Fact is, boy, I wouldn't know what cards was good and what wasn't. It's just a lot of paper to me. And those ball players, paper heroes most of 'em."

It was a good thing that Grampa didn't collect, I thought. Otherwise I might have a hard time getting Dad's cards away from him.

"Grampa, is your suitcase locked?"

"Nope."

"Grampa, you were taking a chance. It's got a 1952 Mickey Mantle card that's worth $2500."

"Well, maybe you better go check and see if Mantle's still there."

"And Yogi and Willie Mays and Yaz and Pete Rose and the 1962 Roger Maris, and Ted Williams' rookie year and . . ." I chanted names as I ran up the stairs.

The suitcase was on the bed in Dad's study. I undid the straps and flipped the latch and opened it.

Grampa packed neat. Not the way Mom and I stuffed things in when we went somewhere. Grampa folded everything neatly. That was probably 'cause of all the road trips he took when he was a player. Ball players live out of suitcases.

On top was a red bathrobe and shirts and pajamas. Below that were long black socks and underwear and a shaving kit and a sweater and more underwear and shirts, and then I felt the hard shape of the box.

I pulled it out. It was still in the brown wrapping paper. Addressed to Grampa. Insured and registered and taped all around with that shiny packing tape. The return address said *Harris, Kendall Park, New Jersey 08824.*

There was no knife or scissors on Dad's desk. I took the package downstairs.

"I need a knife."

Grampa dug in his pocket and then with a quick motion flipped a small red penknife through the air. I caught it with my left hand.

"Still got those good soft hands, I see."

I laughed. "When I don't pitch, I play short-stop. Me and Rudi Gomez alternate." I started cutting the tape. "But I'm the number-one pitcher. We could have a pretty good team if everyone would show up. We could—"

"Andy, please don't talk while you're using a knife. Look at what you're doing," Mom said.

"I *am* looking, Mom."

I slit the tape and pulled off the wrapping paper and my heart skipped a beat. There was the old familiar green box with Thom McAn Shoes printed on the cover. I pulled up the lid.

On top was crinkled up newspaper. I pulled that out. Next there was a white envelope with Grampa's name typed on it.

"There's a letter here for you, Grampa."

"Bring it here, Andy," Mom said.

I brought Grampa the letter. Below the letter was Dad's big printout. Next were the cards themselves. I removed them carefully. Hurt a card's edge and it loses some value. Tubby taught me that.

There was the big 1962 set, tied together with rubber bands.

Then there were Dad's valuable cards. All in plastic sleeves. I checked quickly. The big 1952s: Berra, Mays, the $2500 Mantle card.

I handled each one very carefully. Especially Mantle.

Next was the 1939 Ted Williams. There were three Ace Super 1971 cards: Frank Robinson when he was with Baltimore, and Carl Yastrzemski and Tony Conigliaro of the Red Sox.

Dad had showed me the prices on those three 1971s. Robinson was worth $200, Yaz $135, and Conigliaro $60. Boy, there was a lot of money in this old shoe box.

I set the 1971s off to one side. Next there were a lot of great oldies Dad had bought or traded for. Marty Marion and Terry Moore of the Cardinals, Cookie Lavagetto of the Brooklyn Dodgers, Carl Hubbell, number 11, with his pants way down his socks, and Fat Freddie Fitzsimmons, both of them pitchers with the N.Y. Giants, though Tubby had a card of Fitzsimmons when he was with the Brooklyn Dodgers. Tubby also had a card of the pitcher he was traded for. Someone named Tom Baker. Tubby had everything. Almost everything.

Next there were some of Dad's brother sets: the DiMaggios: Joe, Dom, Vince. Mort and Walker Cooper from the St. Louis Cardinals;

Dizzy Dean and his brother Paul; Lloyd and Paul Waner, who were Little Poison and Big Poison; Hank and Tommy Aaron; Jim and Gaylord Perry. Matty and Jesus and Felipe Alou.

There were Dad's valuable St. Louis Browns cards. Dad was once a member of a St. Louis Browns baseball-card club.

Dad had some black-and-white cards from the Negro Baseball Leagues. Cool Papa Bell and Josh Gibson and Monte Irvin and a guy Dad said was probably the greatest of them all: Martin Dihigo from Cuba, a second baseman who also pitched and batted .372 and played for twenty-three years. That was before black players played in the majors. Dad said their not being allowed to play was one of the great injustices of all time. I'm glad I wasn't alive then.

Grampa had played before Jackie Robinson. But he had met some of these old black players when they barnstormed after the season was over. He said they were good ball players. Could've been major leaguers except for the color of their skin.

Next were more old white guys: Pie Traynor from the Pirates and Chuck Klein from the Phillies. There were four different Babe Ruth cards, three Ty Cobbs, an Eddie Collins . . . real oldies they were. I put them all to one side.

At the very bottom were a bunch of cards that didn't have photos but colored paintings of players.

The top card was Lefty Grove, a great pitcher. And there was Bill Dickey and someone named Buddy Myer and Bill Terry. Grampa once told me that Bill Terry was the best fielding first baseman who ever lived.

"Was he as good as Keith Hernandez?" I asked him.

"Better," Grampa said.

"I don't think so," I said. I was eight years old at the time. Grampa thought I was very funny.

Grampa could never get over that I was always wanting to compare old and new. He said you couldn't do it. "Been too many changes, boy. Domed stadiums. Shorter fences. Artificial turf. The game's different too. Pitchers ain't expected to go nine innings no more. Too many good relievers around. DH's. Scorin's different. Sacrifice flies. Ball's different."

Grampa knew a lot. He also knew personally a lot of the greats. Like Bill Dickey. The greatest catcher who ever lived, outside of Yogi Berra and Roy Campanella and Mickey Cochrane and Johnny Bench. (Dad had four Mickey Cochrane cards!)

Anyway, to get back to those colored paintings of players. On the back of each card were tips on how to play each guy's position. There were catching tips on the Bill Dickey card, pitching tips on the Lefty Grove card. How to bunt on a Van Lingle Mungo card. Mungo was a pitcher.

The tips were not written by the ball players. They were written by someone whose name I couldn't read. He worked for the *Boston American*. That had to be a newspaper.

The cards were called Diamond Stars and below the tips and the sportswriter's name were the player's stats for . . . let's say 1934. Grampa was ten years old then.

"You better read this," Grampa said. I looked up. He was giving Mom the letter from Helen.

"What's she say, Grampa?" I asked.

"If your mom wants, she'll tell you."

"Grampa, Dad never showed me these Diamond Star cards. Do you know about them?"

"Nope. Don't know anything about your dad's cards. I always preferred flesh-and-blood ball players to paper ones."

I blinked. What a funny thing to say. As if you couldn't be both? Be a flesh-and-blood ball player and collect cards too.

"I bet these are valuable, Grampa."

"Probably are if your dad held on to 'em."

I thought fast. If those Diamond Stars were valuable, maybe Tubby would trade *the* card for them.

I picked up Lefty Grove. "They were put out by the . . ." It was in tiny, tiny letters at the bottom. I read, ". . . National Chickle Company. What's chickle, Grampa?"

"Chicklets . . . gum," Grampa said. He was watching Mom.

Mom put the letter down. She shook her head. "She's something else."

"What'd she say, Mom?"

"She's letting us know that she knows the value of the collection."

"Oh. Well, it was really nice of her to send it then, wasn't it?"

Mom didn't answer. Something was fishy.

"What's going on?"

Grampa stood up. "C'mon, Andy, let's go outside and have a catch. I want to check out your flipper."

"No, Jim," Mom said. "He should know about this. He's old enough to understand."

"Understand what?" I said.

"Andy, your father's will is still being probated."

"What's that mean?"

"A judge and lawyers get hold of it and decide

54

how much money your dad left. After his debts are paid off. And it turns out he had quite a few debts. After that, the judge decides how much Helen gets, her girls, and then you."

I never thought about Dad leaving me money. It was the cards he told me he'd leave me. The cards were all I wanted.

"Did he leave me a lot of money?"

"We don't know yet. Helen is telling Grampa that she's had the card collection appraised and that the value of it seems to be eighteen thousand dollars and—"

"Tubby says it's worth more. Dad said so too."

"It could also be worth less," Mom said. "In fact, it would be to our interest if it was worth less. You see, her lawyer says the collection is part of the estate. So that might be eighteen thousand dollars you won't be getting."

"Suits me."

Grampa laughed. Mom didn't. "I don't think you understand, Andy," she said. "If you trade those cards away, you're trading away money. Or, what's more likely since you don't know a lot about cards, you'll be giving away money."

"I'm not gonna give them away. And I do too know about cards. Not as much as Dad or Tubby or Mr. Kessler but . . ." I remembered something then. A message I was supposed to deliver to Grampa.

"Grampa, Mr. Kessler wants you to call him when you get in."

"I'll call Nate later."

"How'd he know you were coming?"

"I told him I was comin'."

I stared at Grampa. Mom did too.

"What'd you do that for?" I asked.

It was the first time I ever saw Grampa looking a little embarrassed. "Thought it might be a good idea if Nate went over your dad's collection and put a value on it."

"Did you know she was getting the collection appraised?" Mom asked.

"Yep. When I called to ask her to send it along, she said she'd have to do that first. So I put two and two together and that was when I gave Nate the call."

Grampa refolded Helen's letter and stuck it in his pocket. He stood up slowly.

"Let's go throw a ball, boy. I never liked baseball cards. Play the game, I say, don't collect it. My mitt's in the car."

"You brought your mitt?" I asked, astonished.

"Yep. Thought it was about time you and me should be playin' ball again. See you outside."

"Jim," Mom called after him, "should you be doing this?"

"Yep, Miss, it's exactly what I should be doin'."
He went outside.

"He brought his mitt with him, Mom. I bet he would coach us if I asked."

"You're not to ask!"

She said it so firmly, I was kind of taken aback. "OK. OK."

I got my glove out of the closet and dug in the athletic box for a baseball. "Wasn't he funny about baseball cards? I thought maybe it was only his own card he didn't like. But he doesn't like any baseball cards."

"No, he doesn't," Mom said.

I found an old Little League baseball. I pounded it into the pocket of my glove.

"You know, it must've been rough on Dad, collecting baseball cards with Grampa feeling that way."

"I think it might have been," Mom said.

"Dad must've been pretty tough in his own way."

"He probably was . . . in his own way."

"You know, Mom, I wish I could have known Dad when he was a kid. I bet we would have been good friends."

Mom smiled. "I think so. Now don't keep Grampa waiting, Andy. And don't make him stretch or run for balls."

"I won't."

Grampa was waiting under the maple tree. He had his old first baseman's mitt.

"Stand over there and throw easy."

He pointed to where I should stand. Just past Mom's rosebushes.

He wasn't worried about himself. Just about my arm. He was worried about me; I was worried about him. I guess that's the way it should be.

I took aim and carefully lobbed one over the rosebush. It was low. Grampa scooped it smoothly off the ground.

"Sorry," I said.

"Sorry for what?" he snapped, and flipped the ball sidearm just over the roses to me. Right at my chest. Smooth and accurate and easy to catch. Grampa threw a light ball. Even when he threw hard, it never hurt.

"Sorry for making you bend."

"Bendin's good for me."

Aim at his head, I thought. I threw high carefully. This one he had to reach over his head to snag.

"Sorry," I said.

"What's all the sorries for, son?"

I blurted, "Mom said not to make you reach for the ball."

"So that's why you're aimin' it. And that's why you're throwin' wild. You're not bein' natural. Just throw it, Andy. You'll be on target."

I winged the next one without thinking. It came in chest high. Perfect. What a good coach he'd be for us.

"Does it hurt you to throw?" I asked.

"Nope. Don't hurt me to catch neither." He smiled. "Only thing that hurts is knowin' I can't hit a curve ball no more."

I laughed the way he wanted me to. "I bet you could hit my curve ball, Grampa."

"You throwin' curves already?" He flipped one between the rosebushes. It had some zing on it.

"Wanna see?"

"Nope."

"Why not?"

We were in a nice rhythm. Talking, throwing.

" 'Cause I seen too many kids ruin their arms throwin' curves, that's why."

"It ain't that much of a curve, Grampa. Can I throw just one? A little one?"

He laughed. "All right. Just a little one. Move back some. You got to give it room to break."

"I won't need too much room, Grampa. My curve doesn't break an awful lot."

I moved back a little. And Grampa moved back a little on an angle away from the garden bed so I wouldn't be throwing through Mom's roses.

He settled down into a catcher's squat.

"Which way's it goin' to break, boy?"

He asked that with a straight face. He was being funny. I didn't have a screwball. Yet.

I kept my face straight too. "That way." I pointed to our house.

"Let 'er rip," he said.

I stepped on an imaginary rubber. Full windup and came down over my head and let go, twisting my wrist hard as I could. The ball bounced in front and to the right of Grampa. He backhanded it smoothly and flipped it back to me in one motion.

"We used to call that pitch a 'drop,' " he said deadpan.

"Can I try just one more, Grampa?"

"All right, but that'll be it for curves."

"Are you feeling OK?"

He looked annoyed. "I'm feelin' fine. But your coach, bad as he is, won't forgive me if you get a sore arm before the season starts."

"Mr. Cartwright wouldn't know a sore arm

from a sidearm. Grampa, if you come to our practice tomorrow you'd see how awful he is. Would you come, Grampa?"

And there it was. It had just popped out. I'd asked him what I wasn't supposed to ask him. But he looked so good catching and throwing. You could see Ace 459 in every motion he made.

"I think I better stay home with your mom. There's nothing worse than an out-of-town expert comin' in and givin' advice and then leavin'."

I should have let well enough alone, but I didn't.

"You don't have to say anything, Grampa. Just tell me later what you thought and I'll tell the other kids. All you have to do is sit and look."

Grampa laughed. "Now *that's* a good pitch."

"Grampa, if I told everyone you were coming we'd have a full team for practice."

"Let's see that breakin' ball, Andy. I can't stay in this squat more than another ten seconds."

"I promise this one will break right, Grampa."

I toed the imaginary rubber again and looked in for a sign. Grampa wiggled two fingers. I nodded. I gripped the ball against the seams. I went to a full windup. And let it go with a mighty twist.

The ball broke all right. It almost broke our basement window. It sailed ten feet wide of

Grampa and hit up against our house. It bounced off and disappeared in the yew bushes under our picture window.

"Not a batter in the world could've touched that pitch, Andy," Grampa said gravely.

I laughed. "I'll get it, Grampa."

As I ran by him he tousled my hair. We were tight, Ace 459 and me.

It took me a while to find the ball. I found an old hose nozzle and a Frisbee before I spotted it under some of last fall's leaves. While I was groping my way out of the bushes, I heard the squeal of bike brakes. I looked out through the bushes. It was Tubby.

"Hi, Mr. Harris, I'm Tubby Watson. I'm a friend of Andy's. My grampa saw you play at Briggs Stadium."

"Did he?" Grampa said. "Good thing he didn't blink. I wasn't there too long."

I came out of the bushes and gave Tubby a dirty look.

"Hello, Andy," Tubby said cheerfully.

I started to say "I told you not to come over" when Grampa said: "Why don't you two have a catch? I'll watch you for a while and then I'll go on and wash up. Here, son . . . what'd you say your name was?"

"Tubby. My real name's Harold."

"Tubby, huh? Well, they used to call me Nose 'cause of this broken schnozzola of mine."

"How'd you break your nose, Grampa?" I'd always wanted to know that but never had the nerve to ask. Having Tubby here made it easier.

"Fella run into me when I was with Beaumont. He was out too. Here, young man," he said to Tubby. "You can use my mitt."

Tubby's eyes widened. This was the glove that might've tagged out Williams and DiMaggio. Tubby was about to take it and then he shook his head. "Thanks, Mr. Harris, but I better not."

I knew just what made him say that. Tubby's terrible and he didn't want Grampa to see him.

Grampa frowned.

Tubby began to sweat a little. "You see," he said nervously, "we had practice this morning. And we had to work hard 'cause only six of us showed."

Grampa's face relaxed. "Well then, you're a real ball player, Tubby. 'Cause they're the ones who always show up for practice. What's your position, son?"

Tubby shot me a look, begging me not to say anything.

"I'm a catcher."

He didn't say he was our second-string catcher.

"Great position," Grampa said. "Only one facin' everyone. Catcher's got to be a take-charge guy."

I grinned at Tubby. He blushed but recovered. "Did you ever catch, Mr. Harris?"

"Caught about forty games for Beaumont one season."

"I didn't know that," Tubby said, interested. "It didn't say anything about catching on your card."

Grampa looked blank.

"Tubby owns your baseball card, Grampa. Ace 459."

"Oh that. Well, that card and a quarter'll buy you a Sunday paper."

He went into the house.

Tubby looked puzzled. "He didn't seem too interested in his card."

"He's not. He's a real ball player."

"Well, Gary Carter collects baseball cards and he's a real ball player. I've met lots of real ball players who like cards."

"Where'd you meet real ball players, Tubby?"

"At card shows. I've met Milt Wilcox and José Canseco."

"That's not meeting them really, Tubby. They're only there 'cause they're being paid. My dad told me that."

"I know that," Tubby said, pained. "I know

what they get paid too. My dad knows the man who puts on the big show at the Dearborn Hyatt. He told me what Johnny Bench charges."

"What's he charge?"

"Fifteen thousand. And he's an *ex*–major leaguer. Pete Rose isn't playing anymore either and he charges ten thousand."

"What do they do for that kind of money?"

"Nothing," Tubby said. "They sit around and shake hands and say, 'How're ya doin'?' to kids who come up for autographs."

"What a racket."

"It's fair 'cause if you advertise that a major leaguer's gonna be at your card show, you can get five hundred kids and charge admission and make your money back fast."

"You gonna charge admission to your big Swap 'n' Sale?" I was half kidding. But you can never even half kid with Tubby about money.

"It's Swap 'n' Sell, not Swap 'n' Sale. And I would charge admission if I could get a major leaguer to come. It'd be OK with my dad."

"Hey, you're serious."

"I told you, Andy. Baseball cards are my game. Like they were your dad's. Listen . . ." His eyes got small again. "When do you want to trade?"

"Any time. Right now. What do you want for it?"

His eyes narrowed even more and I knew I

65

sounded too eager. I'd make a lousy business-man.

"The Mantle card," he said.

"Tubs, that card's worth $2500. Grampa's card is worth twenty-five cents." I decided to try a different tack. "You ever hear of Diamond Stars?"

"Sure. They were put out by the National Chickle Company."

Tubby knew everything.

"Well," I said, "my dad's got a bunch of them. Lefty Grove, Bill Dickey, Buddy Myer, whoever he is—"

"Washington Senators, infielder," Tubby said.

"OK. I bet these cards are really valuable. Tell you what, Tubs, I'll trade you all the Diamond Stars for Grampa's card."

I thought Tubby was going to say no, but he was a businessman. No quick moves.

"Are they reprints?" he asked.

"What?"

"Are they reprints or originals?"

I was going to say "how do I know?" but decided that would be an unbusinesslike thing to say.

"They're originals." I hadn't the slightest idea if they were or not.

"I'll have to look at them first."

"They're in good shape."

"What kind of good shape? Mint? Excellent? Good? I've seen Chicklet cards supposed to be in good shape that were beat up terrible. How many Diamond Stars do you have?"

"About ten or fifteen. I didn't count 'em."

"Let's go in and check 'em out."

"Can't. Mom says no visitors today."

"Why?"

"Grampa's sick."

"He didn't look sick."

"He's come here for tests. Medical tests."

"Well, bring the cards over to the tree house, then. We can trade there. And bring Mantle too," he added casually.

"You gonna have Ace 459 there?"

"Sure. We could swap in two seconds."

"I'll be there."

"When?"

"Right away, I guess."

"Good. Alice Cartwright's coming over in about an hour to trade and I don't like trading with more than one person at a time."

"How're you gonna run a big Swap 'n' Sell show, Tubs, if you don't like trading with more than one person at a time?"

"I won't be swapping or selling at my own show," Tubby said, annoyed. "I'll be running it. You and me today, that's different. That's one-on-one trading. Look, Andy, if you don't want to trade, don't come. I like Ace 459. It's one of a kind."

He got on his bike and took off.

Looking back on it, I realize he was psyching me out. He wanted me to come begging with the Mantle card. And I was ready to.

I went back into the house. Mom was just coming out of the shower. Grampa was lying down in his room. I was standing by his door.

"Mom," I whispered, "can I go over to Tubby's?"

"We're going to eat lunch now."

"But Grampa's sleeping."

"No, I'm not," Grampa called out. "I never sleep in the daytime."

"That's good," Mom said, "because I've got a nice cholesterol-free pasta salad for you."

"I don't need a cholesterol-free anything," Grampa grumped. He got off the bed. "I'm hungry enough to eat a horse."

I laughed. Grampa used expressions you heard on old black-and-white TV shows.

"We'll have a horse for dinner. Go wash up, Andy," Mom said.

And that took care of getting to Tubby's right away. Which turned out to be a good thing because it slowed me down and during lunch, while Mom and Grampa talked, I worked on a game plan for Tubby.

First, I thought, I'd offer him the Diamond Stars for Grampa, and if that didn't work, I'd offer him some of those 1971s, and if he didn't go for that, I'd offer him Ted Williams and Maris and Mays . . . and if that fell through, he . . . could have Mantle.

Some game plan. All I was doing was retreating every step of the way. That was no game plan at all. It was all defense. No offense. A game plan should include putting some pressure on Tubby to trade for a lesser card.

But what pressure could I put on Tubby?

Mom's voice cut into my thoughts. She and Grampa were arguing.

"I don't think you should, Jim. For at least two reasons. One—"

"I may not have many more opportunities, Miss. I can handle myself."

"What're you fighting about?" I asked.

"We're not fighting, we're just discussing," Mom said.

"We're fightin'," Grampa said bluntly. "I've decided I'm goin' to your practice tomorrow."

"All right," I said.

"Couldn't you at least wait till you've taken the tests and heard the results?"

"Miss, I may decide not to even take those tests. They're only excuses for doctors to make money. Nope, I'm goin' to do what I want to do, for a change. I'm goin' to the boy's practice tomorrow."

"And you'll coach him?" Mom asked. There was something ominous in the way she asked that.

"Who said anything about coachin'? If the coach lets me, I'll shake hands with the boys and ask 'em how they're doin'. No more than that. If the coach lets me."

Shake hands with the boys. Ask 'em how they're doin'. Where had I heard those words before?

"We both know you'll do more than that, Jim. And I sincerely doubt that Andy's coach will appreciate being overshadowed by you."

I got goose bumps. I knew where I'd heard those words before. Tubby, a little while ago, imitating what those high-priced major leaguers said to kids at baseball-card shows.

"I can tell you, Miss, at my age, I cast a very short shadow."

And all of a sudden it was clear to me how I could put pressure on Tubs to trade decently for Ace 459. I don't know why I didn't think of it before. Tubby needed a major leaguer to get kids to pay admission to his Swap 'n' Sell. Well, I had the major leaguer right here. I grinned. I now had a game plan going into the tree house.

"Andy," Mom said, "your grandfather just asked you a question."

"Sorry. I was daydreaming."

"Andy, I want you to get your coach's permission for me to attend your practice tomorrow. I won't come unless it's OK with him."

"Oh, it'll be all right with him, Grampa. Mr. Cartwright may not know anything about baseball, but he's a nice man."

"I want *him* to say OK, not you."

"I'll ask him this afternoon, Grampa. Can I be excused?"

"Where are you going?" Mom said.

"Over to Tubby's. And then I'll go over to the Cartwrights'."

"You're going to trade cards at Tubby's?"

"Yeah."

"Andy, those cards are the same as money. Money that's not yours yet. You're not to trade. Do you hear me?"

"I hear you, Mom," I said, grinning at Grampa.

I'd have given anything to tell him about my game plan, but I didn't dare. He was too important a part of it.

7

The funny part was, Tubby would never have had a tree house if it wasn't for my dad.

When my dad was a kid, he built a tree house near where he lived. I saw it on a Sunday about three years ago and told Tubby about it the next day walking home from school.

"What'd your dad do in his tree house?"

"He said he used to go over his baseball cards in it."

"Hmm. Neat. I think I'll ask my dad to build me one."

And that's how Tubby came to have a tree house.

Tubby's tree house was a lot different from Dad's. Tubby's was a palace. It was the Statler-Hilton of tree houses. It had a roof, walls, windows, even carpeting. The only thing missing was an elevator. There was a redwood ladder going up to it.

Dad's old tree house was a few planks of wood nailed together high up in an old oak tree. The walls were the leaves of the trees.

I found out about the tree house back in third grade. It was on a Sunday and Dad, Mom, and I were driving down Pauline Boulevard, which is on the west side of Arborville. Suddenly, Dad pointed off to the right.

"See those woods, Andy?"

"Yeah."

"I built a tree house there when I was a little older than you."

"You never told me you did that."

Mom looked at him curiously. Later, much later, I realized she was wondering why he was telling me this. I guess she knew what it might lead to. I didn't. I don't think Dad did either.

"Well, it wasn't such a hot tree house," Dad said with a laugh.

"You think it's still there?"

"It might be."

"Let's go see if it's still there."

"You really want to?"

"Sure. You want to come too, don't you, Mom?"

Mom shook her head. "I've never been one to revisit the past. I'll wait in the car."

It was a warning to Dad. I didn't know it then.

Dad laughed. "Heck, it's probably not there, Mary. Twenty-six years is a long time. We'll be right back."

Dad and I had to cut through a couple of backyards before we reached the woods. Dad was like a bird dog on the scent. He ran ahead of me pointing out a hickory tree, a black walnut, a locust, a maple . . . pointing out an old log crawling with beetles that had been there when he was a kid. Not the beetles but the log. And then he stopped, looked around getting his bearings, and looked upward.

And laughed. "It's still there."

I looked where he was looking. Halfway up a big old oak tree, where some big branches came together, there were planks of wood.

"That's it?" I said, a little disappointed.

"That's it," Dad said, excited. "Want to go up?"

I shrugged. "How?"

"Climb, man, climb. Let's see if . . ."

He started running around in little widening circles, like a hound dog, peering into bushes, looking for something.

"What are you looking for, Dad?"

"I used to hide an old ladder here in the brush." He laughed. "And here it is."

He pulled a dirty earth-encrusted ladder out of a bush. A rung came off in his hand. He laughed. "Well, that takes care of that and proves one thing."

"What's that?"

"Wood lasts longer in the air than it does in dirt."

He dropped the ladder and walked back to the tree.

"All we need is a leg up," he said. "It's easy climbing after that."

There were limbs coming out every few feet. The hardest part would be jumping up to the first one.

"I think this'll do."

He had found an old stump.

"Give me a hand, Andy."

Together we rolled it over to the base of the tree. It was kind of fun doing this with Dad. We didn't usually do things together. Dad wasn't a ball player or a fisherman. Though sometimes in the spring we flew a kite together.

"I'll test it. If it takes my weight, it will take yours."

He got up and the stump held. He pulled himself onto the first limb.

"OK. All set."

I got up, and he hauled me up with him.

"We're underway," he said, grinning like a little kid. "The trick in climbing is to concentrate,

75

look first, go slowly, think out your moves. Ready?"

"Ready."

"I'll go first. You watch me and then you'll come."

He climbed to the next limb.

"OK, come on up."

From then on I climbed the way he had climbed and he watched me and coached me, from branch to branch, where to set my hands, my feet. Higher and higher we went till, grinning like kids together, we were both on the branch just below his tree house.

"OK. Hold on tight to the trunk. I'll climb up and then help you up."

Dad reached up with his fists and thumped the planks to make sure they would hold us. Then he hauled himself up and lay there on his stomach. Then he turned, still on his stomach, and extended his hand down.

"Grab hold."

I grabbed hold.

"One, two, three . . ." he said.

I pushed off the trunk with my left hand and Dad pulled me up with my right hand, and I was hauled belly down onto the planks. We both lay there looking at each other and then we laughed together.

"We made it," I said.

"We sure did," Dad said. And we slapped palms.

We both sat up and it was a great view. From Dad's tree house you could see over the tops of houses. You could see the football stadium and Ferry Field and State Street and Granger Avenue. You could see clear over to the east side of Arborville where we lived.

Dad looked at the old planks. "You know what I think saved this tree house, Andy?"

"What?"

"The subdivision. It cut off access to the woods. Kids couldn't knock it down. Years ago the woods ran right up to Pauline Boulevard. You could walk right into it. Now it means crossing private property."

"Did you come here a lot when you were a kid?"

"Yeah."

"Did Grampa come with you too?"

Dad looked funny. "No."

"He's so big he'd break the tree climbing up. That's probably why he didn't come with you."

Dad smiled. "Probably."

"What'd you do up here alone?"

"Nothing. Most of the time I'd bring my baseball cards up here and look at them. Sometimes

I just sat . . . and thought about things." He was silent a moment. He had an odd look on his face. "This was my secret place."

"I don't have a secret place."

"You don't need a secret place, Andy."

What a funny thing to say, I thought. I looked at him. And I saw that his eyes were wet. He was crying silently. I looked away. I'd never seen Dad cry in all my life. I didn't know why he was doing it. It made me want to cry too.

"You OK, Dad?" My voice sounded shaky to me.

He took out a handkerchief and blew his nose.

"Yeah. I'm . . . fine. I . . . got something in my eye." He took a deep breath. "Give me a minute, Andy, and then we'll start down. Your mother probably thinks we broke our necks by now."

"What's that building over there? The big white one?" I wanted to change the subject from whatever it was that made him cry.

"That's the American Legion Hall."

"Was that here when you were a kid?"

"Yes."

"Did any of your friends ever come up here with you?"

"I don't remember. Probably not."

"You had lots of friends when you were a kid, didn't you?"

78

"Not too many."

"What about guys on your team? Like when Grampa coached you."

"Andy, that was so long ago I've forgot everything. Listen, I told Mom we'd be right back. We better get started. We've got to be extra careful going down. Most climbers have their falls going down, not up. We'll go down backward, retracing our steps. I'll go first and tell you where to go. OK?"

"OK."

And down we went, carefully, Dad first, and then he'd stop and coach me down, telling me where to put each foot. Down, down, down we went. Slowly, until we were on the last branch. Dad stepped down onto the stump. Then he removed the stump and I jumped down into his arms.

He held me and kissed me. I could still feel the wetness on his cheeks.

"Thanks, Dad. That was fun."

"Thank you for coming with me, Andy. As your mom said, it was a trip into the past."

We walked out of the woods silently.

Mom watched us from the car. She was glad to see us alive and in one piece, she said.

Tubby's tree house has bulletin boards on all
three walls. On the bulletin boards Tubby has
tacked up pictures of ball players, mostly Detroit
Tigers of today and yesterday. Trammel and
Whittacre and Kirk Gibson and Jack Morris;
Al Kaline and Tracy Jones and Denny McLain
and Bill Freehan . . .

That tree house is almost as big as my room
at home.

When I got there that Saturday, I heard a
familiar voice saying in rapid fire: "Got it got
it got it got it got it, don't got it, got it got it
got it . . ."

"Cartwright, you don't got a 1971 Harmon
Killebrew," Tubby said furiously.

Alice was looking at Tubby's cards. Claiming
she had just about everything he had. And it
was getting to Tubs. She could do it, where Kyle
and I couldn't. Partly 'cause she was a girl and
a better ball player than he was. Partly also

'cause she owned a lot of good cards herself.

"I do too got a 1971 Killebrew, Fatty."

"Don't call me Fatty. My name's Tubby. Let's see your 1971 Killebrew."

"It's at home," Alice said with a laugh. She was so tough. Old Tubs would have his hands full cardsharking with her.

"I *bet* it's at home," Tubby said sarcastically.

"How much?"

"How much what?"

"How much you wanna bet?"

If only her father, our coach, was half as tough.

I leaned my bike against the tree and called up: "Hey, I'm coming up."

Tubby's face appeared upside down in the entrance. "You were supposed to be here an hour ago."

"I had to eat lunch."

"You better go now, Alice," Tubby said.

"Go? I just got here."

I climbed up the ladder and slid the green Thom McAn shoe box ahead of me and into the tree house. Tubby's cards were all over the carpet. He'd been putting them down for Alice to see, and she had been putting *him* down with all those "got its."

Tubby left off squabbling with Alice and looked at the shoe box. "Were they all there?"

"Yep."

"When did you start collecting baseball cards, Andy?" Alice asked. She snapped off a bubble.

Alice was one of the few serious baseball card collectors I knew who liked the bubble gum that came with the cards. That's the only way to look at Ace baseball cards. Maybe when Grampa was a kid you bought gum and the cards came with it. Now it's the other way around.

"I don't really collect," I said to Alice. "It's my dad's collection."

"Hey, I heard he had some great cards."

"Okay, Alice," Tubby said with a phony smile, "you and I can trade another time."

"I'd like to see Andy's dad's cards."

"They're Andy's cards now," Tubby said, "and he and I are going to do some trading."

"I won't interfere. Can I see your cards, Andy?"

She had freckles, brown hair, and a stubborn jaw. There was a girl's softball league in Arborville but Alice had got permission to play hardball with us. And hardball was what she played.

I didn't know what to say to her. My game plan didn't include anyone else being present.

Tubby's game plan clearly didn't either.

"Alice, if you want to be invited to my Swap 'n' Sell show, you better go. Right now Andy and I are swapping one on one."

"That's OK. I'll watch," she said with a pleasant smile through a set jaw. She wasn't going anywhere.

Tubby glared at her but he wasn't tough enough to kick her out. I wasn't either.

"We can ignore her," Tubby said to me.

Alice grinned. "Let's see 'em, Andy," she said.

"If you stay, you got to be quiet," Tubby said, trying to sound like he was still in charge.

Alice winked at me and nodded to the box. I had to laugh. It was kind of funny.

I took the lid off the shoe box.

"What's that?" Alice said, pointing to the print-out.

When I told her it was a listing of every card and its value, Alice whistled. "Your dad knew what he was doing."

"Most of us real collectors do," Tubby said, superiorly.

She ignored him. "What're those cards, Andy?"

"That's the whole American League for 1962."

"1962. I got a lot of 'em," she said.

"Will you please be quiet?" Tubby said.

"What else do you got?" Alice asked.

"Diamond Stars. National Chickle Company. With tips on how to play."

"I don't have any of those."

Tubby rolled his eyes helplessly while I showed Alice those colored-painting cards.

"Neat," she said. "Lefty Grove, Bill Terry, Bill Dickey. Hey, let's look them up."

"Listen, Alice, we're not interested in looking up Diamond Stars," Tubby said.

"You call 'em out, Andy. I'll check the prices," Alice said.

She had out her price guide.

Well, why not. This was step one of my game plan. Offer Tubby the Diamond Stars. And then if he was still after Mantle, I'd put on the pressure with Grampa being the major leaguer at his Swap 'n' Sell show. And if I did it right, we'd be back to the Diamond Stars and off Mantle.

"Here it is. Diamond Stars. National Chickle Company. Diamond Stars. 1933, 1934, 1935 . . . shoot 'em at me, Andy," Alice said.

"Lefty Grove, Red Sox."

Alice whistled. "One hundred and forty-five dollars," she said.

Tubby's eyes widened. I think mine must have too.

"Bill Dickey, Yankees."

"Seventy-five dollars. Wow."

"Eldon Auker, Tigers."

"Seventeen dollars. He was the submarine pitcher, wasn't he, Tubby?"

"Yeah," Tubby said, and gave her a dirty look. Which she didn't see, of course.

"Van Lingle Mungo, Dodgers," I said.

"Love that name," Alice said. "Eighteen dollars."

"Schoolboy Rowe, Tigers."

"Twenty-eight dollars."

"Bill Terry, Giants."

"Fifty-five dollars."

"Buddy Myer, Senators."

"Seventeen dollars."

"Heinie Manush, Senators."

"What a name. Sixty dollars."

"Marvin Owen, Tigers."

"Twenty-one dollars."

"That's it," I said.

"That's a lot of money," Alice said. You want to trade some of those?"

"Yeah," I said, looking at Tubby. Tubby was fuming. He didn't want to trade with Alice around.

"I've seen Tubby's cards," Alice said. "He doesn't have anything that good."

"He's got Jim Harris," I said.

"Who's he?"

"My grampa."

"I didn't know your grampa was a baseball card."

"Ace 459," I said.

"Where is it, Tubby?"

I had looked. It was not on the carpet.

Tubby didn't answer her.

"C'mon," she insisted, "where is it?"

"In my pocket."

"Let's look at it."

"It's in mint condition. I don't let anyone touch it."

"All right, you hold it and I'll look."

He took Grampa out of his pocket and held it up. I looked with Alice. There he was: young, tough, raw-boned . . . reaching for a throw from across the diamond.

Alice just stared. It was kind of fun watching someone see it for the first time.

"Ace 459. Jim Harris, first base," she read in a solemn voice. "Let's see what it's worth." She started turning pages.

"We know what it's worth, Alice," Tubby snapped.

"Here it is. Ace 459. Jim Harris, first base. Twenty-five cents." She looked up at me. "A quarter," she said.

"I know," I said.

"Don't trade him a Diamond Star, Andy. They're worth a hundred times as much. Trade him something worth less. Who else you got there?"

"Well, I've got some duplicates. Nellie Fox."

"I've got Nellie Fox up the kazoo," Tubby sneered.

"Just about everything else is worth more, Alice," I said.

I pulled out the next card. It was the 1952 Willie Mays. Alice's eyes widened. She started turning pages.

"Don't bother," Tubby said. "It's a hundred and twenty dollars."

"Is that right, Andy?"

I nodded.

"Boy, what great cards. What's this . . ." She reached for a card.

My game plan was coming apart. I was showing cards to Alice, not Tubby.

". . . Oh, wow, Ted Williams rookie year." She reached for her book.

"Two hundred and twenty-five dollars," Tubby muttered.

Alice was stunned. Well, my game plan was shot, but it *was* kind of fun watching her being knocked over. So I began showing them all to her. One after another. Like ocean waves they came at her. Yogi Berra, Frank Robinson, the Connie Mack cards, Yaz, Tony Conigliaro, Clemente, the Roger Maris home run year, they came rolling at her. And just as she recovered from one, I hit her with another until finally I held up, to Tubby's dismay, the 1952 Mickey Mantle.

Alice stared at it. "I hate to ask."

Tubby didn't answer.

"C'mon, Tubby, what's it worth?"

When he still wouldn't answer but just sat there like a carved miserable fat Buddha, Alice, with a look of disgust on her face, opened the price guide and looked it up and up and up. And when she found it, she was silent. And finally looked at both of us and said: "Two thousand five hundred dollars?"

"Yes," I said.

"So what?" Tubby said.

"So Andy's crazy to be walking around with a card that valuable."

"He's not walking around with it," Tubby yelled. "He's in my tree house trading."

"For what? A card that's worth a quarter?"

"A card's worth whatever someone'll pay for it," Tubby said.

"Tubby Watson, you rat. Andy's your teammate. You ought to *give* him that card."

"I don't give away cards," Tubby said sullenly.

"OK," Alice said, "so which of his cards are you after?"

"It's none of your business," Tubby said.

"Tell you what," Alice said. "You want my 1968 Al Kaline. I'll trade you it for Ace 459."

"Right," Tubby sneered. "So then *you* can trade for his Mantle card."

"So that's what you're after!"

She'd outsmarted him.

"You want a twenty-five-hundred-dollar card for a twenty-five-cent one?"

Tubby's face was red. "I told you, Cartwright. A card's worth what someone'll pay for it."

Alice turned to me. "You wouldn't make that trade, Andy, would you?"

When I didn't answer, she shook her head. "Yes, you would," she said softly. "And that's 'cause you're not a collector. Well . . ." She took a deep breath. "I ain't gonna let you do it."

And then with a move so quick that only a third baseman could have made it, she yanked Grampa out of Tubby's fingers, dropped down through the tree house entrance, and went down that ladder faster than you could believe.

"Hey, stop! You can't do that. That's stealing," Tubby yelled.

Alice was on the ground. She stuck her hand in her pocket. I thought for a second she was going to try to flip the card up to us. So did Tubby. But she didn't take the card out of her pocket.

She took something else out and threw it up through the entrance of the tree house. It was a coin. It hit Tubby on the nose. It was a quarter.

"That's what the book says it's worth and that's what you're getting, Piggy," she yelled, and then she took off.

Next to Kyle, she was the fastest runner on the team.

"That card's worth twenty-five hundred dollars," Tubby screamed after her.

"Not to me," she yelled, and disappeared around the house.

Tubby's cheeks quivered with rage. "She won't get away with that. I'll have her arrested." And then his face grew suspicious. "Did you put her up to that, Andy?"

"No." I said. I put Dad's cards carefully back in the box.

"If you did, you're gonna be arrested too. Neither of you'll get away with it. Where are you going?"

I slid down the hole onto his ladder.

"Over to the Cartwrights'."

"I warn you, if you get Ace 459 from her you'll be receiving stolen property."

"I'm just going over there to ask Mr. Cartwright if it's OK if my grampa comes to baseball practice tomorrow."

"I don't believe you."

"Well, it's true. My grampa's gonna coach our practice tomorrow."

"Really?"

"Really."

Tubby was silent. He was making up his mind about something. Then his jaw set stubbornly.

"I don't care. I'm gonna tell my dad on both of you."

He started picking up his cards. I noticed that he also picked up Alice's quarter.

Kyle and I used to wonder how a wimpy guy like Mr. Cartwright could have someone like Alice for a daughter.

"Maybe her mom's the tough one in her family," Kyle said.

I thought maybe Kyle was right. Mrs. Cartwright had a kind of tough ratty face. She looked fierce just answering the doorbell.

"I'm Andy Harris, Mrs. Cartwright. Is—"

Before I could ask if Mr. Cartwright was home, Alice's seven-year-old brother Jeffrey stepped in front of his mother and pointed at the Thom McAn shoe box in my hands. (I wasn't going to leave it outside with my bike.)

"What's in the box, Andy?" he demanded.

He was Watson Chevrolet's batboy and a class-A pest.

"Jeffrey, don't be rude," Mrs. Cartwright snapped. "If you're looking for Alice, Andy, she's at Tubby Watson's house."

She *was* at Tubby's house, I thought. I wondered where she'd gone with Ace 459. She'd have to return it to Tubby sooner or later.

"Did you hear what I said, Andy? Alice isn't here."

"I came to see Mr. Cartwright, ma'am."

"Oh." That stopped her. "Can I ask what about? I feel my husband's had enough baseball today." She didn't approve of his coaching. Which was OK. None of us did either.

"I bet he's got a guinea pig in there, Ma," Jeffrey said.

"Who is it, Ruth?" Mr. Cartwright called out.

"Andy Harris," Mrs. Cartwright said, biting off my name.

"Great," Mr. Cartwright sang out. "I wanted to talk to him."

"I bet it's a gerbil," Jeffrey said.

Mrs. Cartwright spun the pest away from the door and snapped an unfriendly "Come in" at me.

"What's in there, really, Andy?" Jeffrey asked, twisting out of his mother's grasp.

"It's a rattlesnake," I said.

"Really? Let's see it."

Mr. Cartwright appeared in the front hall. He was holding a newspaper in his hand. He was a tall man with a wispy mustache, glasses.

He looked like a lawyer and coached like one too.

"Hello, Andy," he said with a smile. He meant well.

"Hello, Mr. Cartwright."

"You know what, Dad? Andy says he's got a rattlesnake in that box."

"Is that right? Well, he better keep the lid on tight, then. I'm glad you're here, Andy. I was going to call you this afternoon about tomorrow's practice."

Did he know about Grampa? If so, how? Tubby was the only one I'd told.

"Come into the living room and sit down."

As I went by, Jeffrey poked the box with his finger.

"What are you doing that for?" I said.

"To see if it moves."

"It's dead."

"A dead rattlesnake?"

"Yeah. Rattlesnakes die."

Mr. Cartwright motioned me to sit on a chair opposite him.

The phone rang. "I'll get it, Dick," Mrs. Cartwright said. "And Jeffrey, stop making a pest of yourself."

That was like asking rain not to fall.

"I've never seen a dead rattlesnake," Jeffrey said.

"Jeffrey, did you hear your mother?" Mr. Cartwright said. "If you can't behave, I'm afraid I'll have to send you to your room."

Unbelievable. That was the exact same tone he used in coaching too. "Wally," he once said to Wally Cates, our first baseman, "if you continue to swing at bad pitches, I'll have to move you down in the batting order."

How could you take a coach like that seriously?

Jeffrey looked at me and drew his finger across his lips, letting me know he'd be silent from now on. I didn't smile. You should never encourage a second-grader.

"Andy, we've got a problem with Watson Chevrolet. I just called four of the boys who weren't at practice today: Wally Cates, Ryan Feldman, Tommy Benson, and Calvin Hucker and none of them can come tomorrow either."

Hucker was a sub. But Wally was our first baseman, Ryan our first-string catcher, and Tommy was our left fielder.

"I'm getting concerned," Mr. Cartwright continued. "If we don't get enough kids out for a decent practice tomorrow, we're going to be in trouble on Monday, aren't we?"

"Yes, sir." He was just getting concerned. He was months behind us in concern.

"I wonder if you could help out. The boys respect you . . ."

He stopped. By saying that the guys respected me, he was admitting that they didn't respect him. That was hard. I kind of felt sorry for him. But he shouldn't be coaching.

". . . So I wonder if you could get on the phone and call them and point out how important tomorrow's—What is it, Ruth?"

Mrs. Cartwright's face was grim. "It's Alice. She wants to speak to you."

"Alice?"

"She's calling from a public phone."

"Is there something wrong?"

"I think there is but she wouldn't tell me. She wants to talk to you."

"Excuse me, Andy," Mr. Cartwright said.

"Do you know what's going on, Andy?" Mrs. Cartwright asked me.

"Well . . . I . . . uh . . ."

"Can I talk now?" Jeffrey interrupted. "I bet there's no dead rattlesnake in there at all . . ."

Saved by Jeffrey.

". . . I bet it's a dead gerbil."

Mr. Cartwright's voice in the other room was suddenly sharp and clear.

"Alice, even if you weren't my daughter. If you were just an ordinary client, I would advise you to return it to him. More so since you're my daughter." Silence. "It doesn't make any difference. That wasn't the value *he* put on it and furthermore he wasn't selling it to you. You *stole* it."

Mrs. Cartwright left the room like a shot.

Jeffrey grinned at me. "Alice is going to jail."

And I ought to go from this house right now, I thought. I didn't come here about the card.

"You return it to Tubby and come home right away," Mr. Cartwright said.

"My father has lots of clients who are in jail," Jeffrey added.

"Don't argue. Just do it!" Mr. Cartwright hung up. I'd never heard him shout like that on the ball field.

"What's going on, Dick?" Mrs. Cartwright asked.

"I don't have the full story . . . yet." Mr. Cartwright reappeared in the living room. His face was grim.

"Andy, I just heard a strange tale from Alice. You seem to be involved in it. Perhaps you better tell me what's going on."

He stood there facing me like we were in a courtroom . . .

"According to Alice, you had an expensive baseball card that Tubby Watson wanted. And he had a cheap card you wanted. Is that right?"

. . . and I was the defendant. And all I'd come here for was to see if it was OK with him if Grampa came to practice tomorrow. This was crazy.

When I didn't answer right away, Mr. Cartwright plunged on. "Look here, Andy, my daughter has apparently stolen something. I want to know what it was exactly that she stole. How expensive was the expensive baseball card? How cheap was the cheap one? I want to find out how much money we're talking about." He waited once more.

I didn't know what to say. He was asking about money. As if that was the important thing about baseball cards. Until Alice had butted into Tubby's and my business, money hadn't really been a part of it. It was going to be a straight player-for-player trade between me and Tubby. Whether it was a Diamond Star or Mantle.

"Let's start with the Mickey Mantle card, Andy. What was it worth?"

If he knew what cards were involved, Alice must also have told him what they were worth. But then I remembered from a TV show that lawyers never asked questions they didn't know the answers to. He was building a case.

"Twenty-five hundred dollars," I said.

Mrs. Cartwright gasped. She thought Alice had stolen Mantle.

"And the other card?" Mr. Cartwright asked grimly.

"It's an Ace card of my grampa. It's worth . . . according to the price guide . . . a quarter."

"According to Alice, you were willing to trade your twenty-five-hundred-dollar baseball card to Tubby for his twenty-five-cent one? Is that correct?"

"Yes, sir."

"Why?"

"I want my grampa's card."

He looked at me sharply, trying to decide if I was being honest.

"Alice told me she wouldn't let you trade the expensive card for the inexpensive one? Is that correct?"

I needed a lawyer.

"She didn't say that," I said.

"She said that to me on the phone now. What did she do?"

He clearly knew what Alice had done.

"She grabbed my grampa's card from Tubby and took off."

"Which card did she take?" Mrs. Cartwright asked.

"The twenty-five-cent card," I said.

"Thank God," she said.

"No, Ruth," Mr. Cartwright said, not taking his eyes off me. "I'm afraid it's not that simple.

Alice really took a twenty-five-hundred-dollar card since that twenty-five-cent card now has a value of twenty-five hundred dollars."

"She's going to jail for a long time, isn't she, Dad?" Jeffrey said hopefully.

"She didn't steal it, Mr. Cartwright. She . . . uh . . . gave Tubby a quarter for it."

Though it had been more like throwing than giving.

"And so you came here to buy it from her for a quarter?" he said quietly.

I'd walked into a trap. I stared at him. He had set me up for that. He was building a case that I had been behind Alice. Maybe even put her up to it. Alice was innocent; I was guilty.

I felt a thrust of anger. "I didn't come here to buy a card, Mr. Cartwright."

"Then what did you come here for?"

"My grampa's in town. He wanted me to ask you if he could come to practice tomorrow."

Even as I said it, I knew it sounded like a lie. Would an ex–major leaguer ask permission of an amateur lawyer coach to come to a kids' baseball practice? It sounded so much like a lie to my own ears that I felt myself grinning sheepishly.

The grin put the seal on it. It now also *looked* as though I was lying.

Mr. Cartwright shook his head. "Andy, Alice's

heart may have been in the right place. But her actions weren't. Nor are yours in coming here to buy it from her."

"Mr. Cartwright, I swear to you I didn't come here for that. My grandfather asked—"

I stopped. The look on his face was so disbelieving, there was no point in going on. Why couldn't adults believe you when you were telling the truth? I felt myself getting choked up.

Mr. Cartwright said, "All right, Andy, take it easy. We'll straighten out this mess somehow. And your grandfather . . ." He smiled skeptically. ". . . has my permission to come to our practice tomorrow."

I got up and went to the front door. I didn't get there fast enough. Jeffrey intercepted me. Before I could stop him, he pulled the lid off the box and peered in.

"It's . . . it's . . . baseball cards!" He grabbed one and held it up in triumph. "He did come to trade with Alice!"

I grabbed the card out of his hand and ran out of the house.

10

An opera was playing over the kitchen radio and the lights were on there. Which didn't necessarily mean that Mom was in the kitchen. She had a habit of turning on the radio and the lights in whatever room she was in. And never turning anything off when she left. It used to drive Dad nuts.

"Is that you, Andy?" Mom called from the living room.

"Yeah."

"Alice Cartwright was here a minute ago, and Tubby called a while ago. He wants you to call back."

Mom was sitting on the couch in the living room reading the paper. With no lights on. A kitchen timer was ticking away on the coffee table.

"What did Alice want?" I was really sore at her. She had really screwed up things for me in a royal way.

"She didn't say. But"—Mom reached toward the coffee table—"she left this for you."

My heart thumped. I knew right away what it was. *Ace 459 Jim Harris 1b.*

And there was Grampa. Young and hungry and reaching for the throw from across the diamond. I stared at him.

"How did she come to have it, Andy?" Mom was looking at me curiously.

"She found it in Tubby's hand."

"I thought Tubby sounded pretty upset on the phone. You better call him back now and tell him you have it."

I turned the card over and looked at Grampa's Beaumont stats and his 1945 Tiger stats, and then I looked at the picture again.

"You *will* return it to Tubby, won't you, Andy?"

"No."

"What do you mean, 'no'? You *have* to return it, Andy."

"I'm gonna trade for it, Mom."

"Can I ask what card you're going to give him?"

"You're not interested in baseball cards, Mom. What do you care what card I'm trading?"

"Andy, we've been through this. If you're planning on trading a card from your father's collection, forget it. You can't do it yet."

"When can I do it?"

"When the legal matters are settled."

"When's that gonna be?"

"I don't know. Soon. Whenever there's money involved, things take time. And there's money in those cards."

Money, money, money. That's all everyone thought about. Mom could be the flip side of Mr. Cartwright right now.

"Don't worry, Mom. I've got a game plan and it doesn't involve the cards. It's a way to put pressure on Tubs so he won't want the most expensive card in the collection."

"What's your game plan?"

"Why do you want to know?"

"Because I don't think you really have a game plan. I think you'd be willing to give Tubby the whole collection for Ace 459."

"I wouldn't *ever* do that," I said irately. "Ace 459 is worth a lot, but it's not worth that much. No, I've got strategy and, as a matter of fact, it involves Grampa." And that was as much as I was going to reveal to her. "Listen, when Alice was here, did she see Grampa?"

This was important, because if she had seen Grampa, it would prove to Mr. Cartwright that I hadn't been lying. That Grampa was in town and could show up for tomorrow's practice.

"No, she didn't. Grampa was sleeping. Really sleeping this time. In fact, he's still asleep. He's been asleep for over an hour already. Which shows you that he's not really well, Andy."

"Did you tell her he was here?"

"No. Why would I do that?"

"Because when I was over at the Cartwrights' just now, Mr. Cartwright didn't believe me that Grampa wanted his permission to come to practice tomorrow. He said sarcastically it was OK, but I know he thought I was lying about it."

"Why did he think that?"

"He thought the reason I'd gone over there was to buy Ace 459 cheap from Alice. Just like you, Mom, he thinks cards are only about money."

"Cards are money to a lot of people, Andy."

"I'm not a lot of people. But it's OK." I laughed. "It'll be one in the eye for Mr. Cartwright tomorrow when Grampa shows up and starts coaching. He'll show him up for the lousy coach he is."

Mom didn't say anything. I knew she hated to hear me talk like that, but I was right. Mr. Cartwright deserved whatever he got tomorrow.

The little white timer on the coffee table went off.

"Come with me, Andy."

"What for?"

"I want to talk to you about that practice tomorrow."

That had also been Mr. Cartwright's opening line.

"What do you want to talk about?"

"Come."

I followed her into the kitchen. An opera singer was going full blast. Mom turned off the radio. She opened the oven door and with two mitten potholders took out a pie. She didn't make pies for the two of us. A lot of good was coming out of Grampa's visit. She closed the oven door with her foot and put the pie on a metal rack.

Then she turned to me. She held her hands in front of her and the potholders looked like boxing gloves.

"I don't want Grampa to go to your practice tomorrow," she said.

"Grampa *wants* to come."

"I know he does. And if he could just sit and watch and be quiet, it would probably be all right. But he's not like that and it won't be that way."

She took off the potholders and put them in a drawer and faced me again.

"Those medical tests Grampa's here for concern his heart, Andy. For some time, Grampa's been having chest pains. If he has the kind of heart blockage the doctors up north suspect he has . . ." She stopped.

"Like he could have a heart attack?"

106

"Yes. *Like*," she repeated the word with distaste. (Since Mom was an English teacher in the high school, she hated bad English.) "Like," she repeated, "he could have a heart attack."

I was silent. Every game plan you make, someone tries to wreck. Alice in the tree house grabbing Ace 459. Now Mom making it impossible for me to prove to Mr. Cartwright I was telling the truth.

But even worse than that. We'd have a full team tomorrow if the kids knew Grampa would be coaching them. It was our last chance to start the season on the right note.

"So Grampa shouldn't come to practice at all?"

"That's right," she said.

"Can I be excused? I want to go up to my room."

"Andy, I want closure on this."

"What's that mean?" It was a teacher's word.

"It means I want to accomplish something with this discussion. Will you tell Grampa not to come?"

"How can I do that? What am I going to say?"

Mom was silent a moment. "You could tell him Mr. Cartwright doesn't want him to come."

"That would be lying. Even though he didn't believe me, Mr. Cartwright said Grampa could come to practice."

"Andy, sometimes we tell lies to make things

better. You can't think of them as lies then."

"Yes, you can."

"All right. If you're not able to say that, I'm sure you can find some other way to talk Grampa out of coming to your practice."

"Like what?"

"Well, you could tell him that *you* don't want him to come."

"That would be a worse lie. That would be the worst lie ever. Can I go now?"

"Yes. And . . . thank you."

"For what?" I said bitterly.

"For looking after your grandfather. And Andy . . ."

"Now what?"

"Don't forget to call Tubby back."

"For Pete's sake!"

"And one more thing . . ."

I froze. Now what?

"When you're talking with Tubby about the card . . . will you please remember that your dad's baseball cards are money that doesn't belong to you yet. You're not to trade, Andy. Will you remember that?"

I'll say this much for my mother. She touches all bases.

"I'll remember," I said bitterly.

11

Grampa was lying on his back, breathing in and out regularly. He looked old and thin asleep. His Adam's apple bobbed up and down. His neck looked scrawny.

I closed his door and went into my room.

I propped Ace 459 up on my desk. Then I opened the shoe box and took out Dad's printout. I found the computer entry for Mantle.

$2500.00   1 Mickey Mantle $0.00

The phone rang in the hall. I ran to get it before it woke up Grampa. It only rang once. Mom had got it. I waited a second, and then I heard her footsteps in the back hall.

"It's for you," she whispered up the stairs. "Is Grampa still sleeping?"

I nodded.

"Move the phone into your room," she whispered.

"I will," I whispered back. I carried the phone into my room and shut the door.

"Hello, Tubby," I said.

"What're you calling me Tubby for?" Kyle said. "What'd I do wrong?"

"I'm hanging up now," Mom said into the other phone.

"I thought it was Tubby. I'm supposed to call him back."

"Don't waste your time," Kyle said. "He won't be there. He called me to find out where you were. He told me the whole story, Andy. He and his dad are going over to the Cartwrights' now. Alice is in trouble all right."

"She doesn't have the card, Kyle. I do."

"Huh?"

"She left it here while I was out."

Kyle laughed. "I guess you're both in trouble now. But, heck, even if they arrest you both, we'll still have plenty of kids for practice tomorrow. Tubs told me your grampa was gonna coach us tomorrow. I called the Gomez twins and they're calling the other kids. Including the subs. Andy, we'll have all the starters and all the subs at the park tomorrow."

I felt sick. Kyle went merrily on.

"We'll have enough kids for a practice game. Heck, even my mom wants to come, Andy. And she never comes to our real games. She's comin' to get your grampa's autograph."

In his room Grampa stirred. I felt like crawling under the nearest bed.

"You there, Andy?" Kyle said.

"Yeah."

"Will your grampa give autographs?"

Grampa was moving around in the room.

"I . . . uh . . . I gotta go, Kyle," I said, and hung up.

I put the phone back. Grampa's door opened. He stood there with sleep all over his face.

"I'm sorry about the phone ringing, Grampa."

"That's all right. I shouldn't be sleepin' in the middle of the day. We had a rookie at Beaumont used to sleep in the dugout between innings. Couldn't hit worth a lick awake. Andy, I got a call from Nate Kessler. He can look at your dad's cards this afternoon. How about I borrow 'em for about an hour?"

"Sure, Grampa. They're right here. Can I ask you a question?"

"Depends about what."

I laughed 'cause he wanted me to.

"My friend Tubby. You remember him?"

Grampa smiled. "I remember Tubby."

"He's a big baseball card collector. This summer he wants to put on a baseball-card show in his backyard. He needs an ex–major leaguer to be there to say hello to kids and give autographs. I was wondering, if you were still here, would you do it?"

"Do what?"

"Say hello to kids and give autographs at his baseball-card show. I bet he'd even pay you something."

"You serious, son?"

I blushed. "Yes."

Grampa's face got grim. "There's not a chance in the world I'd ever do anything like that, Andy. I don't think ball players and baseball cards go together. I know there's some ball players that'll do anything for money, but I'm not among them. Never was. Never will be."

He went off to the bathroom. My face burned. Well, that took care of what was left of my game plan. I couldn't deliver Grampa. Tubby would get Mickey Mantle now, no questions asked.

I took Mantle out of its sleeve and put Grampa in. Then I put Grampa in the box next to Mays and Berra, and I put Mantle in my pocket.

Finally, I crossed out Mantle's name on the printout. And wrote in Grampa above it so it all looked like this:

| $.25 | 1 Jim Harris | ~~$0.00~~ |
| $2500.00 | 1 Mickey Mantle | ~~$0.00~~ |

I hesitated for a second about putting the printout back in the box, but it would be unfair to Mr. Kessler not to. So I did.

Grampa was coming out of the bathroom.

"Here're the cards, Grampa."

"You ask your coach about my comin' tomorrow?"

There it was. I hadn't expected it that fast. It was like being quick-pitched. I had to swing in a hurry and I did.

"Yeah." I couldn't meet his eye. "He'd rather you didn't come."

Grampa's face fell. I could have died.

Then he sort of hitched himself up. "That's OK. I'll catch you in a regular game soon as I get through with these darn tests."

He walked slowly down the steps holding the Thom McAn shoe box. I heard him tell Mom he was going down to The Grandstand for a while.

After he left, Mom came upstairs.

"Did you . . ."

"Yes," I yelled at her. "I lied and hurt his feelings."

She looked at me understandingly. "I'm sorry, Andy. But you did the right thing. And I thank you for it. If he could, Grampa would thank you too."

I didn't answer. I brushed by her.

"Where are you going?"

"To trade Mantle for Harris."

"You can't do that, Andy," she shouted at me.

"I'm going to," I shouted back. "You can't win them all, Mom."

12

"Andy!" Alice yelled.

I was halfway across the park, biking past a little kids' practice on Diamond One. I turned around.

Tubby was with her. They were both on bikes. My first piece of luck. Now I wouldn't have to face Mr. Cartwright so soon.

"Hey, get off the field," the right fielder shouted at me. They were third-graders having batting practice. I was in deep center field. Maybe Mark McGwire could hit one this far.

"He can't hit it this far," I said, and started pedaling toward Tubby and Alice.

"Hit it out here, Tony," the kid yelled.

The pitcher pitched a terrible pitch and Tony missed it by a mile.

"See?" I said.

"Stay there," the right fielder said to me.

I laughed and biked over to Baldwin Avenue, where Alice and Tubby were.

"I was on my way to your house," I said to Alice.

"We were on our way to yours," Alice said, grinning a little. For someone in a big jam, she seemed pretty loose.

Tubby, on the other hand, wasn't grinning at all. He was glaring at me. I decided to cheer him up.

"I was going there to find you, Tubs," I said.

"What for?" he snapped. "You already got my card."

"Yeah, here it is."

I took Mantle out of my pocket.

Tubby didn't even look at it. "Keep it," he said sullenly.

"Hey, this is a trade. This is the card you're after, isn't it?"

He looked at the card in my hand for the first time and saw it wasn't Jim Harris but Mickey Mantle.

"Don't you dare take that, Tubby Watson," Alice said.

"He *wants* to trade it."

"Tubby," Alice said softly, ominously, "if you take that card, I'm gonna bike over to your house and tell your dad."

Tubby was silent. Then he shrugged. "You can keep your grandfather's card, Andy. I don't

116

want it anymore. He was only in the big leagues one season anyway. I don't want him in my collection. And I don't care if he's gonna coach us tomorrow; I'm not gonna be there. I'm quitting the team. And you'll probably have to get a new sponsor."

With that, Tubby jumped on his bike and took off.

I was flabbergasted. Alice shook her head. "The rat. He was gonna take Mantle from you at the last second. His father would have killed him. And don't worry about him quitting the team. His father won't let him do that either."

"I don't understand what's happening."

Alice looked at me surprised and then she laughed. "That's right. You weren't there. You don't know."

"Don't know what?"

"What happened."

"That's what I'm asking you. What happened?"

"Sit down and I'll tell you."

We got off our bikes and sat in the grass in deep right field, well beyond the range of any third-grade Mark McGwire, and Alice told me what happened at the Cartwright house when Tubby and his father went to look for the "stolen card."

*   *   *

Some of it happened before Alice got home, and she learned that part from Jeffrey.

It seems that right after I left the Cartwright house, upset because they thought I was a liar, Mr. Cartwright went to the telephone.

"Who're you calling?" Mrs. Cartwright asked.

"The Watsons. I want Conroy Watson to know I'll get that card back to his son."

"Are you scared of Mr. Watson, Dad?" Jeffrey asked, troublemaker that he was.

"No, I'm not scared of Mr. Watson, Jeffrey," Mr. Cartwright said quietly. "But I believe I owe him the courtesy of a phone call in this matter. . . . Hello. Is Mr. Watson there? Do you know when he'll be back? Oh. I see. Thank you."

He hung up. "They're on their way here now. Sometimes I wonder about this whole baseball business, Ruth. Me coaching, Alice playing and collecting cards. I could cheerfully shoot her."

"I bet you couldn't," Jeffrey said.

"Jeffrey, you're not even close to funny," his mother said. "You better go upstairs."

At that moment, though, Jeffrey spotted Tubby in front of their house.

"Tubby's here," he announced.

"Is his father with him?" Mr. Cartwright asked.

"No. Tubby's on his bike. Wait. Stay tuned. Here comes a big white car."

"That's him. Conroy Watson drives a white Cadillac."

"There's no police car with them," Jeffrey reported.

"That's it," Mrs. Cartwright said. She told Jeffrey to go to his room. He sort of shot up the stairs. He didn't go into his room, though. Not Jeffrey. He stayed in the hall and eavesdropped, lying on the floor and peeping through the bannister.

Tubby's father, Mr. Watson, the owner of Watson Chevrolet and every other business in Arborville, is kind of a legend in Arborville. He's a large man with tiny eyes. For some reason, tiny-eyed big men scare people. Everyone was scared of Mr. Watson.

Tubby was scared of him. Which is why he played baseball.

Mr. Cartwright was scared of him, which is why he coached baseball. At least, that's what I thought.

Mr. Cartwright opened the door.

"Hello, Conroy. I was just calling you."

"Dick. Mrs. Cartwright."

Mr. Watson took off his hat and bowed politely to Mrs. Cartwright.

"Won't you sit down, Mr. Watson?"

"Conroy, ma'am. I believe we've met at some of the games."

"Conroy, I'm sorry about this baseball card mess," Mr. Cartwright said. "I'm sure Alice will be able to explain everything once she gets here. She'll return Tubby's card."

Mrs. Cartwright said, "Can I get you something to drink, Mr. Watson? Conroy. Tea? Coffee? Tubby, would you like a soft drink or a glass of milk?"

Tubby's eyes darted around the room. "Where's Alice?"

Mr. Watson looked sharply at Tubby. "Harold, I believe I heard Mrs. Cartwright ask if you would like a soft drink or a glass of milk?"

"Uh . . . no, thanks," Tubby mumbled.

"A cup of coffee would be fine, ma'am. Black. No sugar."

"We're expecting Alice any second," Mr. Cartwright said. "About what she did, Conroy, we really don't understand it at all."

"It's not hard to understand," Tubby said furiously. "She stole my card so she could sell it to Andy Harris. Andy came here, didn't he?"

"He was just here," Mr. Cartwright said.

120

"When he didn't find Alice here, he made up a story about his grandfather being in town and wanting to help coach our team tomorrow."

"Oh, he didn't make that up," Tubby said. "His grandfather *is* here and wants to come to our practice and help coach us."

"What?" Mr. Cartwright was stunned.

"His grandfather's here and wants to come to practice and help coach us," Tubby repeated.

"Oh, dear," Mr. Cartwright said.

"I think you owe the boy an apology, Dick." Mrs. Cartwright said, bringing in a tray with three cups of coffee on it. Watson got the first cup.

"Thank you, ma'am. Seems to me it'd be mighty nice having an old major leaguer help you coach, Dick. Not that I think you need a lot of help."

Mr. Cartwright laughed. "I do all right. I know my limitations."

"It's a wise man that does. On the other hand, when no one was willing to coach, you were there. And that counts for a lot in my book. But frankly, I'd like to see Watson Chevrolet do a little better this year. When the newspaper lists the standing of teams, I'd like to see Watson Chevrolet on top instead of on bottom for a change. Be good for business."

121

Mr. Cartwright laughed again. "Be good for my self-esteem too. I'd love to have Andy's grandfather help us out."

"Dad, we came to get my card back," Tubby reminded him.

"Well, we did at that, didn't we? What about Harold's card, Dick?"

"I told Alice to come right home with it," Mr. Cartwright said. "I don't know what's keeping her. She—"

"Here she comes," Jeffrey shouted without thinking. No one even looked up the stairs at him. They all looked to the front door.

Alice came in chewing bubble gum.

Tubby jumped up. "Where's my card?"

"I gave it away, Fatso."

"Alice!" Mr. Cartwright said angrily.

They both ignored him. "What do you mean, you gave it away? Who'd you give it to?" Tubby was angrier than Mr. Cartwright.

"I gave it to Andy. But he wasn't home. I left it with his mom." Alice looked around and seemed to be noticing Tubby's father for the first time. Her mouth fell open.

"You weren't entitled to do that," Tubby said. "It wasn't yours to give away."

Alice said weakly, "I gave you a quarter for it."

"You threw a quarter at me. And it hit me in the face. I could have lost an eye."

"Maybe you should have. It might improve your hitting."

"All right. That will be enough out of you, young lady," Mr. Cartwright said.

"Let me get this straight, little lady," Mr. Watson said quietly. He had been watching without any expression on his face. "You say you threw a quarter at Harold—"

"That's what the price guide says the card is worth, Mr. Watson."

"And then you *gave* the card away?"

"Well, it's Andy's grampa, and he wanted the card. And Tubby was going to make Andy trade him a Mickey Mantle card worth twenty-five hundred dollars for it. His father left him that card. His father died last Christmas. Andy would've given Mantle to Tubby too because he wants his grampa's card so bad. It's not fair for Tubby to do that."

"Who says it's not fair?" Tubby shouted at Alice.

"Harold . . ." Mr. Watson said softly. And Tubby shut up. "Harold, did you drag me over here for a twenty-five-cent card?"

"It's worth twenty-five hundred dollars, Dad."

"Is it?"

123

"Aren't you always saying that a car's worth what someone'll pay for it?"

"That's true. But this is a card, not a car, son. And the customer in this case happens to be your friend. Fact is, to my way of thinking, any boy willing to give up twenty-five hundred dollars for his grampa could make for a mighty fine friend."

"Dad," Tubby wailed, "I don't just want the '52 Mantle 'cause it's expensive. I want it 'cause I don't have it."

What Tubby's dad didn't understand was that Tubby was a collector. In addition to being greedy.

"Harold," Mr. Watson sighed, "I hate to tell you this, but there's lots of things in this world folks want but can't have. And there's things in this life folks want and should have. Like their grampa's baseball card. Especially if that grampa is going to coach you tomorrow. Harold, do you still have this young lady's twenty-five cents?"

Tubby nodded, looking unhappy. He knew what was coming. He felt it was unfair. And, in a way, it was.

"Good. You hold on to it. Folks, it sounds like we've finished all our business. Harold's got his money. The Harris boy has got his grampa's card. Our coach is going to have an assistant

124

tomorrow. The young lady here has to feel good about bringing off the deal, and I am surely grateful for a fine cup of coffee. Good day to you all."

Out the front door he went. Tubby, stunned by the turn of events, sat there in a daze.

Alice went over to him. "Hey, I didn't know Andy's grampa was in town and was going to coach us."

Tubby looked at her. "He's not gonna coach me," he said. And got up and left.

"Wait up. I'm going with you," Alice called after him.

"Alice, I think you've made enough commotion for one day," Mr. Cartwright said.

"Dad, I just wanna make sure he tells Andy he can keep both cards. And I'd like to meet his grampa too."

"Can I go too?" Jeffrey called down the stairs.

"What are you doing up there?" his folks yelled at him.

And that was how Alice came to be with Tubby when I met them at the park. They were biking to my house while I was biking to theirs.

"That's quite a story, Alice," I said when she finished.

"Now you can see why Tubby's sore."

"Poor old Tubs. In a way, I feel sorry for him."

"I don't," Alice said. "He's such a pig. I don't see how a man as nice as Mr. Watson could have such a pig for a son."

It was almost the same thing Kyle and I used to say about her and her father.

"Maybe Tubby's mother is mean," I said, grinning.

"Probably," she said. "So how about it, Andy? Can I go over to your house and meet Ace 459?"

Only Alice, besides me, would call Grampa Ace 459. "He's down at The Grandstand now. He and Mr. Kessler are going over my dad's collection to put a price on it."

"You better put that Mantle card back in it, then."

She was right. I hadn't thought of that.

"I'll go down there now and do it."

"Can I come with you?" she asked.

"Sure." I owed Alice that and a lot more. I owed her both Grampa and Mickey Mantle. "Come on."

It was only after we got on our bikes that I realized what a dumb thing I'd done to let her come with me. I had lied to Grampa about Mr. Cartwright not wanting him there tomorrow. If the subject came up, Alice could give the lie to my lie.

But it was too late to stop now. We headed for The Grandstand.

13

Two kids we knew from Sampson Park School were just leaving The Grandstand when we arrived. At least I thought they were leaving.

"Don't bother to get off your bike, Harris," one said, "the store's closed."

"It can't be closed," I said, wishing it was true.

"Well, the door's locked and there's a sign on it," the other said.

"A nutty sign too," the first kid said.

"Let's see a nutty sign," Alice said. She biked up to the entrance and started laughing.

"It *is* a nutty sign, Andy. Come look."

On the window part of the door there was a small hand-lettered notice that said:

CLOSED FOR BUSINESS

"Mr. Kessler's the only man in the world who'd close his store for business," Alice said.

It was funny all right, but I didn't laugh. I knew what the business was. Mr. Kessler was

127

going over Dad's twenty-thousand-dollar collection and didn't want to be interrupted by a kid buying forty cents' worth of bubble gum.

I didn't tell Alice that. It was a break for me. "Let's go," I said.

"Wait. I see a light in the back." Alice was on tiptoe peering over the notice.

"He always leaves a light on when he closes up," I said. "Let's get out of here."

"No, there's definitely somebody there. It's Mr. Kessler. And there's another man. Hey, I bet the other guy's your grampa."

Only Alice Cartwright would call a man of sixty-five a guy.

She pounded on the door. "Hey, Mr. Kessler, open up."

"You're gonna break the glass. We can come back later."

"He's looking this way."

"I'm leaving." I got back on my bike.

"He's coming this way, Andy."

"I'll see you later."

"Can't you read English?" Mr. Kessler's sour voice floated onto the sidewalk.

It was too late to leave. Alice was saying, "Andy Harris is here, Mr. Kessler. He wants to give his grampa another card."

"Where is he?"

"Right there," Alice said.

Mr. Kessler peered around the corner and spotted me. I felt trapped.

"Where's Ace 311?" Mr. Kessler demanded. A great greeting.

"Oh," Alice chimed in, "that's the card Andy's putting back in his dad's collection. Ace 311 is the 1952 Mickey Mantle." Alice was all information and help.

"I know what the card is," Mr. Kessler said grumpily. He never took his eyes off me. "Why did you cross it off the printout?"

I'd forgot about that.

Alice had the answer, though. And, of course, she was right.

"Andy was gonna trade it to Tubby Watson for his grampa's card, but"—she grinned— "Tubby gave him his grampa's card."

Mr. Kessler looked at her and then at me, and it was the first time I'd ever seen him come close to looking surprised. He knew that Tubby Watson *never* gave away anything.

"Well," Alice said, with a laugh, "the truth is Tubby's dad *made* him give Andy the card. Mr. Harris is gonna coach Watson Chevrolet tomorrow."

All right, I thought. That's enough. From now on, be quiet.

"What's goin' on, Nate?" Grampa called from inside the store.

"Couple of kids trying to pull the wool over my eyes," Mr. Kessler said. "And one of them belongs to you."

"Send Andy in, would you? I want to talk to him."

My only hope now was that Mr. Kessler wouldn't do it. That he was still "closed for business." But Ace 459 had spoken, and Mr. Kessler just motioned us in.

Here we go, I thought, drifting toward a dangerous waterfall.

We followed Mr. Kessler past the candy and the magazines and the paperback books and the newspapers and the baseball stuff—cards, caps, pennants, napkins, caps—into a small back room that had a table, a sink, a small refrigerator, a hot plate, an old-fashioned electric adding machine, Dad's cards, and Grampa.

Alice stared at Grampa. I don't think she expected to see such an old-looking man.

Grampa was holding a baseball card. I couldn't tell what it was. Those ball hawk-blue eyes took in Alice and then they turned on me.

"You didn't do anything dumb, Andy? Like trade that expensive 1952 Mickey Mantle card for this?"

He slapped Ace 459 down hard on the table.

"No, I didn't, Grampa," I said, wishing he'd

be more careful with his own card. I set Mantle down gently, next to Ace 459.

Grampa looked at the Mantle card and turned to me. "So how'd you come up with the card, Andy?" He knew how long I'd been on its trail.

I didn't really want to talk about it, but this was a safer subject than the one I was afraid would come up.

So while Mr. Kessler pushed buttons on his adding machine, checking out prices in the print-out and two price guides, and examining each card carefully, I told Grampa what had happened in Tubby's tree house and then what Alice told me had happened in her living room with Tubby and his father.

Grampa looked at Alice closely. "You grabbed this card from Tubby, Miss?"

Alice nodded. She still hadn't said a word. She was too awed to talk.

Grampa shook his head as though it was all too much for him. "Girls ain't what they used to be, Nate."

"She's our third baseman, Grampa," I said.

"Sounds like she can handle the hot corner all right."

That broke the ice for Alice. She found her tongue.

"We're all pretty excited about your coaching

us tomorrow, Mr. Harris. Especially my dad. He doesn't really know too much about baseball."

And so it happened. Always faster than you think. We were going over the falls right now. Hold on tight, I told myself.

"Wait a second, Miss," Grampa said. "Say what you just said again."

In a second I'd be drowning. I closed my eyes.

Alice repeated what she had just said.

Grampa said, "Your dad *wants* me to come to practice tomorrow?"

"You bet! Didn't Andy tell you?"

Silence. The only sounds were the *click, click, click*s of Mr. Kessler's stupid old adding machine.

I opened my eyes. Those hard blue eyes were fastened on mine.

"I'm sorry," I whispered.

Alice looked bewildered. But that didn't matter now.

Click . . . click . . . click . . . went Mr. Kessler's adding machine.

Grampa looked at me the longest time. Then he turned to Mr. Kessler. "How long you think we'll be, Nate?"

"Forever, if I keep on being interrupted."

Grampa took a deep breath. "All right then, we'll talk about it later, Andy."

"Lock the door behind them," Mr. Kessler snapped.

The *click, click, click*s followed us back through the store.

Alice went out the door first. As I started to leave, Grampa grabbed my arm with fingers of steel.

"Was lyin' to me your idea or your mother's?"

When I didn't answer right away, the grip tightened.

"Mom's," I whispered.

His grip relaxed.

"But Grampa, I want you to coach us tomorrow more than anything in the world."

Those blue eyes could penetrate to the bottom of your soul. Did I mean that? Yes, I did. I wanted to cry out: I'm a ball player too, Grampa! Your kind of ball player.

Perhaps Grampa heard my silent cry. The grim lines in his tough old face flattened out. "Son," he said, "I want to coach you too."

He let me go. He went back to the *click, click, click*s of Mr. Kessler's adding machine. I went outside, where Alice was waiting.

14

"What's going on?" Alice asked.

"Nothing." We started biking home.

Unlike Tubby, Alice was in good shape. I couldn't leave her behind.

"Your grampa looked surprised that my dad wanted him to coach."

"Well, you know how it is. Sometimes pros think they're not welcome."

"You told him he was, didn't you?"

"Sure." Once you tell your first lie, a second one follows easily. Luckily for me, Alice started talking about letting everyone on the team know. She talked about that all the way to Sampson Park, where we parted. She went left to Baldwin Avenue and Wells, I cut across the park to our house.

"Anybody home?" I yelled.

The house smelled of a good Saturday-night dinner. I knew about the pie.

"I'm upstairs," Mom called.

I went right up. I had to warn her. She was at her desk typing.

"What're you doing?"

"Writing a letter to Uncle Larry. How did it go with Tubby?"

Tubby, I thought, was the least of it now.

"I gave him back the card but he wanted me to keep it."

She stopped typing. "I don't believe that."

I had to laugh. "It's true. There was no trade. I get to keep Ace 459 for nothing."

"That does not sound like Tubby Watson."

"It isn't. His dad made him."

I told Alice's story to Mom. Her reaction didn't surprise me. I'd felt the same way at first, but not now.

"It wasn't fair of his father to make him do that," Mom said.

"Yes, it was."

"No, it wasn't. It was Tubby's card, not his father's. Mr. Watson sounds like a bully."

"A good bully, though."

"There's no such thing. Where's Grampa now?"

Here we go. Only this would be a tiny waterfall compared to the one at The Grandstand.

"He and Mr. Kessler are still going over Dad's cards. Mom, Grampa knows I lied about tomor-

135

row. Alice was with me and she told him her dad was happy he was going to help coach us."

Mom winced.

"I'm sorry. It just came out. I couldn't stop Alice."

"This means he'll be coaching you tomorrow?"

I nodded.

Mom was silent. "I guess it can't be helped. Was he mad at you?"

"He asked me if it was your idea to lie. I had to say yes."

Mom sighed. "Of course you did. It was the truth. It *was* my idea. And now I've been caught out. Well, I'll survive your grampa's wrath, but I hope you and he survive tomorrow's practice."

"Mom, he doesn't have to leave the bench to show us things. And me, Rudi, or Kyle can demonstrate for him. He won't get a heart attack. And if he does, Wally Cates' father is a doctor. He'll probably come to practice. A lot of parents'll be coming. Even Kyle's mom is coming." I laughed. "Can you beat it, she wants Grampa's autograph."

Mom smiled.

"Are you gonna come?"

"No."

"Why not?"

"Why not?" She paused. "I'm not coming because, Andy, if what I think might happen does happen, I don't want to be there to see it."

"For Pete's sake, he won't get sick tomorrow."

"That's not the only thing I'm worried about."

"What else is it, then?"

Mom started looking for the right words. When you're an English teacher, you get picky.

"Well," she said, finally, "there's a chance you may not like your grandfather as a coach."

Crazy words she found. I'd have laughed, but I didn't want to hurt her feelings. "Mom, he played major league ball. He coached high school ball in Arcadia. He's gotta be a great coach."

"I'm not talking about his knowledge of baseball. Or his experience. I'm thinking of something that goes hand in hand with having been a professional athlete."

"What's that?"

Mom looked for the right words again. "Let me put it this way. Your grandfather is a competitor."

"What's the big deal about that? He couldn't have got to the major leagues without being a competitor. I'm a competitor too. Grampa and I are exactly alike."

"In some ways you are. But in other ways you're very much like your father."

"Not as far as ball playing goes, Mom. There

I'm Grampa through and through. Even if I don't turn out to be a first baseman. Which is OK 'cause lots of major league fathers and sons played different positions. Tubby's got a whole bunch of father-son cards. Yogi Berra caught. Dale Berra played shortstop. Bob Kennedy—"

"Stop! The last thing I want to hear about are father-and-son baseball cards. Especially since we were talking about a grandfather and a grandson. Listen, I think we've discussed the subject enough. And I do want to finish this letter before Grampa gets back."

She started typing again. I watched her and thought about what she'd just said. She was right, of course. It was grandfathers and grandsons we were talking about. I wondered if there were grandfather-grandson baseball cards. Or even three-generation cards. Grandfather, father, grandson. There could be. Baseball's been around a long time. Tubby would know. But Tubby wouldn't be talking to me for a while.

Talk about three generations. Over Mom's head, on the wall, was a picture of me, Dad, and Grampa. I'm sitting on Dad's lap. I must have been about two years old when the picture was taken. Grampa is standing behind Dad, his big hands on Dad's shoulders. Mom said she took it up at Arcadia. It's a nice picture. I'm glad it's still up.

One thing I've noticed is that when people get divorced, pictures disappear. They disappeared in Grampa's house in Arcadia. There used to be a bride-and-groom photo of Mom and Dad on the mantel next to a picture of Grampa and Grandma on *their* wedding day. Grampa and Grandma in their wedding clothes are still there, but Mom and Dad have disappeared.

"Mom, can I ask you something?"

"No," she said, typing.

"You remember that wedding photo of you and Dad that Grampa and Grandma had on the mantelpiece?"

"Yes." Her hands paused.

"You think he's still got it?"

"I don't know." She went on typing.

"I wish he didn't take it down."

"*Hadn't taken* it down."

"You know what I mean. Why'd he do that?"

Mom stopped typing. She looked at me. "Well, I think your grandfather took our divorce pretty personally. And that goes back to what I was saying a moment ago about Grampa being a competitor. He doesn't like to lose."

"What's losing got to do with your divorce?"

"I think Grampa counts our divorce as one for his loss column."

"That's crazy."

"I'm not sure it is. I think the real reason

your father married me was because Grampa approved of me as a wife for him."

"Now that *is* crazy. You were in love with Dad when you got married, weren't you?"

"Very much so." She half smiled. "I *also* approved of your father marrying me."

"Dad was in love with you too, wasn't he?"

"I don't know," she said.

That shocked me. "Mom, I'm talking about before he fell in love with Helen."

"I know what you're talking about, Andy. And the answer is: I don't know. When you get married, Andy, you inherit a lot of unfinished business. And I think I inherited a lot of unfinished business between your father and your grandfather."

"Grampa loved Dad. I know that."

"Yes. He did. But I'm not talking about love. I'm talking about approval. I'm not sure Grampa ever approved of your father. And I think Daddy wanted that approval more than anything else on earth. It could not have been easy growing up the son of a local legend, a great athlete, especially when you're not particularly athletic yourself. Marrying me was one way for Daddy to get Grampa's approval."

It was one of the few times Mom had referred to Dad the way she had before the divorce. "Daddy." It made me feel good.

"OK, Mom, but if marrying was one way for Dad to get Grampa to approve of him, wouldn't getting divorced be a sure way to lose that approval? Why would he want to do that?"

Mom looked surprised that I had thought that out. She smiled. "Good point. Unless . . ."

She was thinking it through. And suddenly it was exciting. We were really talking to each other. I'd never ever talked like this with her. Most conversations you have with your parents are sort of set out ahead of time. You're a kid; she's your mom; the words fall between you like they're supposed to. But here we were, Mom and me, thinking out loud together.

"Suppose, Andy, marrying me hadn't worked, and nothing had changed between Daddy and Grampa. He still hadn't got Grampa's approval and, God rest his soul, he still needed it. Then, divorcing me was no problem. What do you think?"

"It's still no reason to get divorced."

"Well, maybe by divorcing me and marrying a woman his father didn't particularly approve of, maybe by doing that he was finally able to cut the tie to Grampa. Maybe in the end, Andy, your father wasn't so much divorcing me as divorcing Grampa."

I shook my head. "If that's what happens when you get married, I'm never gonna marry."

Mom laughed. "You'll get married someday, Andy, and let's hope it's to someone who won't make up elaborate excuses for her shortcomings as a wife."

"Hey, you were a great wife to Dad."

"Thank you, Andy Harris. Now how about letting me finish before—"

But it was too late. We both heard the Buick pull up in the driveway.

"There goes my letter. Thanks a lot, Andy."

"Finish it. I'll talk with Grampa."

"Thanks," she said. And this time she meant it.

15

I opened the door for Grampa. "Did you and Mr. Kessler finish?"

It was a dumb question. He had the shoe box in his hands. "Where's your mom?"

"Upstairs. What did Mr. Kessler say the collection's worth?" I took the box from him.

"Fifteen thousand eight hundred dollars."

"That's impossible. Dad said they were worth at least twenty thousand dollars."

"Fifteen thousand eight hundred dollars is a lot of money, son. It's a lot more than I got in the bank in Arcadia."

"That's not it, Grampa. It's like Mr. Kessler is saying Dad didn't know his baseball cards. He did!"

Mom came down the stairs.

"Miss, you and I have—"

"Something to discuss. I know, Jim, but first I want to make sure that fifteen thousand eight hundred dollars is a figure that can be sent to Helen?"

"It's all here." Grampa took an envelope out of the inside pocket of his jacket and handed it to Mom.

"What's that?" I asked.

Mom opened the envelope and took out two pieces of paper. "It's a letter from Mr. Kessler. Here, this is a copy." She handed me one of the papers. I read:

THE GRANDSTAND
1297 Packard Road
Arborville, Michigan 48104

I have examined the baseball card collection of the late James Harris, Jr., comprising 912 cards. Using *The Baseball Card Digest* as the source for price/value, I put a value of $15,800 on the collection.

Nathan Kessler
Proprietor
6/12/89

Grampa sat down on a straight-back chair. "He says to send the original to her." "Her" was Helen. Grampa would never mention her name.

Mom said, "Well, it looks pretty official."

"It's not official," I said. "Does this mean Mr.

Kessler would only give me fifteen thousand eight hundred dollars for Dad's cards?"

"Andy, would you please not forget that it's to your interest if the collection is worth less." Mom took the copy from me.

"It's still an insult to Dad," I said.

Grampa looked at me, amused. "If that is really botherin' you, Andy, I believe Nate Kessler might give you a bit more for the cards."

I stared at him and then I laughed. "I knew it! I knew it was worth more. Mr. Kessler cheated for us, didn't he, Grampa?"

"Cheatin's maybe too strong of a word. Maybe Nate thinks if you were to resell the cards individually, he might get you close to twenty thousand."

But there was a grin in those hard blue eyes. And I knew then that Mr. Kessler *had* shaded things our way. He'd do it for Grampa. Businessmen always do things for ball players. That's the way it is.

Mom put the envelope in the mail drawer by the staircase. "Well, whether it's fifteen thousand or twenty thousand, I suppose now I'll have to increase the fire insurance on the house. We probably ought to buy a safe, too."

"Cool. If you get a big safe I could put my trophies in it too. I've only got three so far, Grampa. But if we win our baseball league I'll get a baseball trophy. We should have the best sixth-grade basketball team this fall, and if we win that—"

Mom interrupted me. "There's an old expression, Andy. Never count your trophies before they're won. Now, how about you going upstairs and putting the cards away? Your grampa and I want to talk alone for a minute."

As I took off up the stairs, I heard Grampa say, "There's the difference between the two of 'em right there. Jamey collected cards; Andy collects trophies."

"Is that so different?"

"You buy cards, Miss. You earn trophies."

"Jamey earned his cards," Mom said.

I paused at the top of the stairs.

"You know," Grampa said, "I'm real surprised you still stick up for him after what he did to you."

"And I'm surprised you still put him down after what you did to him," Mom said.

I didn't understand that. And I didn't want to. I ran into my room and put the box of cards under the sweatpants in my closet. But before I did, I removed Ace 459 and stuck it carefully in the frame of my bulletin board.

"There you are, Grampa," I said to Ace 459. "And there you'll stay."

Then I started back downstairs. They were now talking about my lying to Grampa.

"I asked him to do that to protect him as much as you," Mom was saying.

"I know what you think you're protectin' me from, Miss. But what in God's name do you think you're protectin' Andy from?"

I sat down on the top step. Jeffrey the Pest Cartwright had nothing on me as far as eavesdropping went.

"You know perfectly well from what," Mom said. "Andy idolizes Ace 459."

I got goose pimples.

"The way Jamey once did," she added.

"I see," Grampa said. And then his voice was so low I had to lean forward to hear. "I know what you're worried about, Miss, but you can quit because Andy's not Jamey. They ain't the same kind of kid."

"They're more alike than you think, Jim."

"Nonsense. They're night and day. Just to start with, Andy doesn't give a fig about money. And that's all Jamey cared about."

"It wasn't all Jamey cared about, Jim. But it was something he found he could be good at. Something you weren't even interested in."

"And I'm still not, Miss."

"I'm not sure I'd be proud of that, Jim."

"I'm not proud of myself, Miss. I know who I am and what I've done in life. And what I haven't done either. If I'm proud of anything, it's of your boy's values. His bein' willin' to trade a twenty-five-hundred-dollar card of Mickey Mantle for a quarter one of his old grampa. That means something to me, Miss. That's the only kind of medicine I need. They say genes skip a generation. He's got my genes all right."

"Andy's not like you, Jim. He's a good athlete all right, but he's not you inside. He's not tough the way you are."

"You're tellin' me he's not a competitor? Baloney. I say the boy is."

"Well, if he's such a competitor, why did you avoid coaching him all these years? Why did you avoid even coming to his games? What were you afraid of, Jim?"

Grampa chuckled. "Well, Miss, to tell the truth, I *was* a little doubtful about his character. I was afraid deep down he might be a card collector too. But I know different now. By gum, I do. Mantle for Harris, is it? There's no card collector in the boy. He's all ball player.

"And secondly, Miss, something else. This health business of mine. Fact is, I *don't* know how much time I got left now. While I'm able, I want to work with him. I want to coach him. I want to help him with everything. Skills, physical conditioning, all of it. I want to give him routines for push-ups, sit-ups, stretches, wind sprints. Kids don't do this stuff today. They want shortcuts. There are no shortcuts to the top. I want to help Andy make it, Mary."

"What's 'it,' Jim?"

"*It*, Miss, is havin' your face on a bubble gum card a lot longer than I did. *It* is being worth more than a quarter someday."

"Oh, Jim," Mom said, "what an awful trip to lay on a little boy."

That got me mad. First of all, I wasn't so little, and second of all, that was a trip I wanted to take. The big leagues. My own face on a bubble gum card one day. I stood up; the step creaked. They stopped talking.

"Andy?" Mom called.

"Yep," I said, and thumped down the stairs. "When are we gonna eat? I'm hungry. I could eat a horse."

Grampa laughed.

16

And finally it was Sunday.

Mom and I went to church. Grampa stayed home and read the papers. Practice was scheduled for one. It was a little after twelve when Mom and I got home from church.

"Ready to go, Grampa?" I yelled, running up the stairs to change.

"I thought you said practice was at one."

"I wanna get there early."

Grampa laughed. "You got the right idea there. But these old bones'll rest up with the paper. I'll be there soon."

"Diamond One *at* one," I yelled down the stairs.

It was a great day for a practice. A blue sky, and a breeze that sent white clouds blowing from west to east over the school and the big old elm trees that lined the park.

As I ran by the tennis courts, I heard two tennis players complaining about the wind.

"This is impossible," one said.

"It's impossible for me too," said the other.

In the middle of the park a father and son were doing the right thing with the wind. They were flying a kite. Dad and I used to fly kites when I was little.

In the spring the big old elms were "kite" trees. Dad used to call them that because they snagged kites. Every spring you could always see three or four kites dangling from branches like large, strange, colorful flowers.

On Diamond One, three second graders were playing ball. One was pitching, one was batting, and one was at shortstop, daring the batter to "hit one out here."

I sat down on the first base side bench to put on my baseball shoes. The pitcher stopped to watch me. That's how serious they were about playing.

"You gonna play here?" the pitcher asked me.

"Yep," I said.

"What's the name of your team?"

"He plays for Watson Chevrolet," the batter said.

"We're the Sampson Park Tigers," the pitcher said.

"Come on, Raymond," the kid at shortstop yelled. "Pitch the ball."

"Take it easy, Claypool." Raymond pitched a

ball that bounced up to the plate. The kid swiped at it with his bat and missed. The ball rebounded from the backstop. The batter picked it up.

"Throw a strike, Raymond," he said, and threw it back six feet over Raymond's head. It skipped by the shortstop, who was watching me lace my shoes.

"Wake up, Claypool," the pitcher yelled.

"I'm awake," Claypool yelled, and chased it and threw it back on one bounce to the pitcher, who missed it. It rolled past the backstop and almost to the parking lot.

"You guys are pretty sad," I said.

"We're terrible," the pitcher said. "Is Tubby Watson on your team?"

"Yep."

"I live next door to him. I've been in his tree house."

"So've I."

I lay down and started doing push-ups.

"What're you doing that stuff for?" the batter asked me.

"It's good for your upper body," I grunted.

"Maybe we should do that too," Raymond said. "Our upper bodies stink."

"Our lower bodies stink too," said Claypool, the shortstop.

They gathered around to watch me.

"Your name's Andy Harris, isn't it?" Raymond asked.

"Yep."

I started doing sit-ups.

"Our coach doesn't make us do that stuff."

"Neither does ours," I grunted.

"All our coach tells us to do is wake up."

"Sounds like our coach."

"Here comes your team."

"Where?"

"Over there."

I turned and looked where they were looking. Across the park came Watson Chevrolet, some on bikes, some trotting to keep up. There was Kyle on his bike; there were the Gomez twins walking, and Wally Cates, Joey Angelo, Tommy Benson, Calvin Hucker, Steve Carlson, Jerry Cohen, Stan DiMasso, Ryan Feldman . . . some of those guys had stopped coming after the first practice. They were all coming back! The word was out about Ace 459 coaching today.

"Is that your coach?" Claypool asked.

He was pointing to the parking lot. Mr. Cartwright and Alice and Jeffrey were getting out of the Cartwright station wagon.

"Yep." I kept on with my sit-ups.

"Ugh, there's Jeffrey," the batter said.

"You guys know Jeffrey?"

"He's in our class."

"Is he on your team?"

"Naw. He just collects baseball cards."

"That's what Tubby Watson does in his tree house," Raymond said.

Mr. Cartwright had got the trunk open and was hauling out the equipment bag. Jeffrey was headed our way.

"What are you guys doing here?" Jeffrey asked the second graders.

"Playing ball," Raymond said.

"Well, you got to quit playing. We're having a practice."

Jeffrey was a pest even to his own classmates.

"You don't play for Watson Chevrolet, Cartwright," Raymond said.

"I'm the batboy," Jeffrey said proudly.

"So what," Raymond said.

"Andy, man," Kyle shouted. He had sprinted and was ahead of the others. I noticed he still had Don Baylor and Rick Burleson flipping between his spokes.

"Where's your grampa?" he said, skidding to a stop inches from me.

"He'll be here soon."

The rest of the team came up.

"Where's your grampa, Andy?"

"He'll be here soon," Kyle said.

154

"About time you came to a practice, Cates,"
I said.

Wally grinned. He was a big lazy kid but a
good athlete. He was our first baseman.

"And you too, Feldman."

Ryan Feldman was our first-string catcher.
He grinned sheepishly. "I was sick this morning, Andy."

The guys laughed, quietly, because Mr. Cartwright wasn't that far away. He was stacking
Alice's arms with batting helmets and shin pads,
and she already had a bat and her glove. Mr.
Cartwright couldn't even pack a bag right. All
that stuff should fit in the bag. Alice kept dropping a helmet.

"We could have enough guys for a game," Joey
Angelo, our second baseman, said.

"Where's Tubby?" someone asked.

"He quit the team someone said."

"No kidding."

"That's the first good news we've had this
year."

"Will his dad sponsor us anyway?"

"No way. His dad'll make him play."

Kyle grinned at me. "I heard you got *the* card."

I nodded.

"Way to go." He punched me lightly on the
arm.

"Who told you?"

"Alice."

"Someone ought to help Alice with the gear," Rudi Gomez said, making no move himself.

"Hey, Jeffrey, you're the batboy," Kyle said. "Go carry those helmets for your sister."

"I'm a batboy, not a helmet boy."

"If that kid was my little brother he'd be dead," Tommy Benson said under his breath.

I went over to Alice and grabbed two helmets.

"Thanks. Where's your grampa?"

"He's coming."

"What's so good about his grampa?" one of the little kids asked Jeffrey.

"He's Jim Harris," Jeffrey said.

"Who's Jim Harris?"

"He's on an Ace bubble gum baseball card."

"Really?"

"Here comes the fat one," Ricki Gomez said.

"Tubs has rejoined the team," Kyle said with a laugh.

"Looks like he went free agent," Benson said.

"And signed for big bucks," Kyle said.

The guys laughed. Tubby was being delivered to the park in his dad's white Cadillac.

"Jeffrey," Mr. Cartwright said, "set out the bats. OK, boys . . . Loosen up. Andy, is your grandfather here?"

"He's coming, Mr. Cartwright," said about four guys at once.

"Can we have a practice game, Mr. Cartwright?" Ricki Gomez asked.

"I don't know. Andy's grandfather is going to coach us today, and it's up to him." Mr. Cartwright came over to me and said quietly, "I owe you an apology, Andy."

"That's OK." I was embarrassed. I'd never been apologized to by a grown-up before. I grabbed a ball and looked for someone to play catch with.

Tubby walked by me. He didn't look at me.

"You want to throw with me, Kyle?" he asked.

Usually Tubby and I loosened up because we were friends and he was a catcher.

"Sure, Tubs," Kyle said with a wink at me. "Nice of you to give Andy the card."

"I didn't give it to him," Tubby snapped, and walked away from Kyle too.

"Is that him, Andy?" Ricki Gomez said.

I looked toward the parking lot. Grampa was coming toward us. Walking slowly but tall and erect. Wearing a baseball cap, a windbreaker, and carrying his old first baseman's mitt and a pair of baseball shoes. Real ones, real spikes.

Everyone stopped throwing.

17

Mr. Cartwright cleared his throat. "Would you introduce me, Andy?"

"Sure."

It was funny in a way. Mr. Cartwright, a lawyer with ten times the money Grampa had, being nervous about meeting an old major leaguer. It told you something, didn't it?

"Grampa, this is my coach, Mr. Cartwright."

Grampa stuck out a big hand. "Nice to meet you, Coach."

Mr. Cartwright laughed. "Thanks for calling me that but it's an exaggeration. The boys are looking forward to having you work with them, Mr. Harris."

"The name's Jim. And I'm lookin' forward to workin' with them too. It's kind of you to invite me."

"How did you want to start the practice, Mr. Harris?"

"You do what you always do, Coach. I'll just watch for a bit."

"Keep warming up, boys," Mr. Cartwright called out to us.

It was a wonder no one got hit on the head, because just as each kid threw or caught, he glanced over to see if Grampa was noticing him.

Grampa was on the bench putting on his spikes. (Mr. Cartwright wore tennis sneakers.)

After he got them laced up, Grampa walked around, looking at people.

"What's your name, son?"

"Steven Carlson, sir."

"Shift your weight forward when you throw, Steven. You want to get something on those throws. What's your name, son?"

"Rudi Gomez."

"That's a nice easy motion you got."

"And this is Rudi's twin brother, Ricki," Mr. Cartwright said.

"Glad to meet you, son."

"My daughter Alice."

"How's the hot corner, young lady?"

"I'm guardin' it," Alice said, and snapped off a big pink bubble as she whipped off a throw to Ryan Feldman. She put some sting into it for Grampa.

Grampa smiled. "I guess you'll do."

He studied Ryan and his big catcher's mitt.

"I take it you're a catcher, son."

"Yes, sir."

"Let's see you throw without movin' your feet."

Catchers often don't have time to take a step into the diamond when a guy's stealing second.

Ryan snapped a swift one back to Alice.

"That's the stuff," Grampa said.

"This is Tubby Watson, our second . . . our other catcher," Mr. Cartwright said.

"Tubby and I are old friends, aren't we, son?"

Tubby nodded uneasily.

"Snap your wrist at the top of your throw, son. You'll get accuracy, and after you put some years on you, you'll get steam too. Bein' a catcher, you need that snap throw arm or they'll run a merry-go-round on you. That's it. That's the ticket. Keep peggin' the ball like that."

Tubby's face flushed with pleasure. He looked around to see if the other guys had heard.

"I guess you know Andy Harris," Mr. Cartwright said.

"I've seen him around."

Everyone laughed. And the introductions went on.

Grampa coached even while being introduced. While saying hello to Fred Hirth, he spoke to Art Castleton.

"You're holdin' your glove wrong on those low

throws, son. Hold it up. That way if you do bobble it, it'll stay in front of you. Andy, toss me one in the dirt."

I threw one at Grampa's feet, glad Mom wasn't here to see this. Everyone stopped as Grampa short-hopped it like it was nothing at all and came up ready to throw. Everyone saw the smoothness. Him being old, it just brought out his smoothness even more.

What Grampa didn't know, of course, was that little Art Castleton couldn't catch a ball with a bushel basket.

After about fifteen minutes of warming up, Grampa had us put our gloves down.

"We'll loosen up our bodies, gentlemen," he said, and that was when we started doing knee bends and push-ups.

Grampa did them with us for a few seconds. I couldn't believe he'd do that, but there he was. I looked around to see if Dr. Cates had come yet—some other parents had—but he hadn't. On the other hand, Mom hadn't either.

We did about ten push-ups each and they were hard. Then sit-ups. As I did my sit-ups, I saw that those little second-graders were still there, watching openmouthed. They were getting all kinds of free lessons today.

After the sit-ups Grampa showed us stretches we could do that would stretch our calf and thigh muscles. We supported ourselves on one leg by holding on to another guy's shoulder.

It was like big time. There was a sense of order to the practice. Someone was in charge who knew what he was doing.

After the stretches Grampa announced we would do some wind sprints. He looked around the park and decided the warming shelter was about the right distance.

"To that little building and back. We'll have some races."

He was making a contest of it, which could make it fun.

He counted out three groups of six. And we had footraces. Kyle won his group. Alice won hers. Tommy Benson beat me in my group.

Then the winners raced and Kyle won, Alice was second, Benson was third.

After that, we ran slowly around the bases, following Grampa. He took a wide turn at first, and as I took my turn right behind him, I looked at the sidelines. Lots more parents had arrived and were setting up lawn chairs. There were little brothers and sisters there too. Kyle's mom was there with a pad and pencil. My mom wasn't. Nor was Dr. Cates.

"This is like spring training in Florida," Brian Seitz behind me puffed. "This is fun." Brian was a sub. I'd never heard him say anything like that before.

After we ran the bases a couple of times, Grampa announced batting practice.

"Five swings and a bunt, and you run out the bunt just like it could be an inside-the-park homer. Even if it's foul, you run it out. Infield, you can make a play on the runner. Runner keeps goin' no matter what. All the way around the bases. No slidin'. Just runnin'. No tags. Just runnin'. Coach, pick a battin' order and set the bottom half in the field and then start rotatin' 'em."

Grampa had done more talking and moving than I'd seen him do in a long time. He was breathing hard. I walked over to him as casually as I could.

"You OK, Grampa?" I asked as quietly as I could.

Those ball hawk-blue eyes gleamed. "Never felt better in my life, boy. How about you throw to the first three batters?"

"Sure."

"This is battin' practice now. The object is to let them hit. Who's up, Coach?"

"Kyle's up first," Mr. Cartwright said. "Alice, you're on deck. Rudi's in the hole."

I tried not to laugh. Mr. Cartwright was the

163

opposite of Grampa in how they talked. Mr. Cartwright used baseball expressions. Grampa said real stuff.

Ryan was going to catch for half the team, Tubby for the other half. Grampa stood halfway down the third base line and watched closely.

I lobbed fat pitches in. Kyle hit a couple of grounders to the left side.

"You're pullin' off the ball, son. Keep your head down. Your eye on the ball. It's a simple business. You see it. And when it gets to you, you hit it. Battin's natural."

Kevin hit a liner into the outfield on the next pitch. I think it was luck. But it established Grampa as a genius right away.

After Kyle ran out his bunt, Alice batted next and popped up to third. Grampa shortened her swing. "Choke up a little, Miss. You don't need that big of a swing. What you want is a quick bat, get it around faster. You won't be lungin' at it that way."

Alice, who popped up a lot, hit a ground ball between third and short.

"There's no one right way to bat for everyone. You bat who you are," Grampa said.

Rudi Gomez was up next. Rudi swung with a choked bat to start with. Grampa didn't change that. But he told Rudi to move up in the box.

On my next pitch, Rudi hit the ball over his brother Ricki's head in left field.

It was different from any practice I'd ever been involved with. Grampa had tips for each kid. Real specific ones too. Like:

"Get your left elbow up higher, son."

"You're droppin' your shoulder, fella."

Grampa was funny too.

"Don't bail out, son. He won't hit you. And if he does, why he couldn't do damage in a greenhouse."

Everyone listened because there was something in it for everyone. Especially about fielding. Grampa talked about the importance of paying attention on every pitch, anticipating, moving on the crack of the bat, keeping grounders in front of you, throwing ahead of the runner, knowing where you were in the ball game, where the runners were, who was fast, who was slow, how many outs there were. There was the importance of knowing the count at all times, seeing how the batter's feet were positioned. Was a guy swinging late or early? Where was your pitcher throwing? How fast was he throwing?

"You can give yourself a break in this game," Grampa said over and over. "You can know what's gonna happen before it happens."

He had great tips for Wally at first. How to

move his feet. The importance of not getting frozen into a stretch too soon.

Mr. Cartwright relieved me at the pitcher's mound when Tubby's turn came to bat.

Tubby, who lunged at pitches, was a terrible hitter. He struck out an awful lot. Well, Grampa watched Tubs miss a couple of pitches and then he moved into the batter's box with Tubby and told him to sit down.

"On what?" Tubby said.

"On this invisible chair I'm settin' below your fanny. There you go. Get your butt down. That's good. You won't fall. I'm holdin' you. Now shift your weight from your rear foot to your front and back again, and do it again and back again. That's right. Now as you shift your weight forward, bring your stick around slowly. Not too hard, or you'll hit your battin' coach. How's that feel?"

"Terrible," Tubby said.

Grampa laughed. "Coach, toss us one and we'll see if he hits as bad as he feels. I'll tell you one thing, son, you won't be able to lunge out of that stance."

Mr. Cartwright threw. It was wide, but Tubby reached out from his weird-looking sitting position and poked it into right field.

A cheer went up. That cheer was for Tubs. But it meant something else to me too. It meant we were becoming a real team. Cheering for each other. Grampa was molding a team out of a bunch of kids who usually couldn't care less.

"It feels better," Tubby said. "Thanks, Mr. Harris."

And that's how batting practice went. Everyone got a tip of one kind or other. Except, I've got to admit, me.

I can hit pretty good. I'm not bragging. I lashed Mr. Cartwright's first pitch into center field on a line. I hit one to left and then I shifted my feet slightly and hit it into right. Grampa watched me like a hawk. When I was done, just before my bunt, he said: "That's good hittin', Andy."

I bunted down the first base line and ran the bases. As I rounded first base, Wally Cates said, "He's been coaching you, hasn't he?"

"Not really. He's never even seen me play in a game."

"You're kidding."

"No," I shouted back.

"Don't talk while you're runnin' bases, Andy. What you do in practice is what you'll do in a game. All right, son, step in there."

And the batting tips went on.

What was really nice was the way Grampa coached everyone. Kids who were ball players and kids who were not. He acted like every kid on Watson Chevrolet was capable of making the major leagues.

At one point Kyle whispered to me, "Now we know what it's like to have a real coach."

After everyone had their five swings and a bunt, Grampa gave us a bunting clinic. He demonstrated what he called "the lost art of buntin'." He showed us how to wait till the pitcher had committed himself, and then square around, move your hand up the barrel of the bat and then, as the ball made contact, pull it back slightly, so it wouldn't go too far out into the diamond. How to shift feet. To bunt down the first base line. Bunt down the third base line.

Then we had bunt, run, and field practice. Everyone had a chance to move a runner to second. Everyone had a chance to be the runner. And Ryan and Tubby had chances to throw out the runners. And Rudi and I alternated at shortstop and Joey Angelo played a tough second.

It was organized and terrific. Along the sidelines the parents were watching in silence. The silence was a real tipoff. Usually the parents talked to each other during the games. Now they were quiet, watching. A practice! It was fantastic. And Mr. Cartwright was watching too. He was awed by Grampa!

There was still more to come. It was like Grampa was trying to cram it all into one session. But that was fine with us. Who knew if there would be more sessions?

Base running. Grampa showed everyone how to make the turn at first, hit the inside part of the bag. Grampa demonstrated that himself. He didn't run hard. But he ran. Again I was glad Mom wasn't here to see.

Grampa also demonstrated sliding techniques. The hook slide away from the tag. How to come in with one leg tucked under you so that you'd be coming up ready to keep going if the ball got away from an infielder.

Grampa didn't actually slide. He lay down on the ground and showed how your body should look as you came in.

"If a play's near close, always slide. If you're in doubt, slide. Gettin' tagged out standin' up is . . . is unforgivable."

Everybody had a crack at sliding. It was amazing how kids as uncoordinated as Castleton and Seitz caught on to it.

"How about headfirst slides, Mr. Harris?" Ricki Gomez asked.

"Don't do 'em, son. First of all, you got young heads. You don't want to get them creased. Second, you don't want to get your hands stepped on. Third, nine times out of ten your head won't get you there any faster than your foot."

"How do we slide if the catcher's blockin' the plate, Mr. Harris?" Kyle asked.

"You don't slide, son. You knock him over. That's your right and his risk. The base path belongs to the runner. Knock him down. He'll live and the ball will be knocked loose."

Grampa spat. A major league spit. Better than Len Dykstra's spits used to be on TV.

"OK, what do you say we put all this high-priced instruction together and play a three-inning game?"

"All *right*," everyone said. Even the subs. Even the guys who were terrible, who were being forced to play by their parents, wanted to play now.

"Coach, you appoint two captains and then I'll show you how we picked sides when I was a kid playin' sandlot."

"Sounds good to me," Mr. Cartwright said, and chose me and Rudi Gomez as captains.

"OK," Grampa said. "It'll be the Andys against the Rudis. Andy, toss this bat at Rudi. Rudi, you catch it and then the two of you go hand over hand to the top and the guy who gets the last grip, and it's got to be a good grip, gets first pick. Toss it, Andy."

I tossed the bat at Rudi. He caught it around the middle. I put my hand over his, his over

mine, mine over his, his over mine, mine over
his, his over mine, mine over his, and then there
was about a half inch of handle left. Rudi held
it by his fingertips, looking pretty grim.

"You got a good grip, Rudi?" Grampa asked.

"I got a great grip," Rudi said through clenched
teeth. Everyone laughed.

"Prove it by whirlin' that bat around your head
three times."

You could have heard a pin drop as Rudi, his
tongue sticking out as he concentrated, slowly
twirled the bat around his head three times.
When he did it, everyone cheered. Including me.

Grampa looked at me, surprised.

"Do I get first pick, Mr. Harris?" Rudi asked.

"You sure do, son."

Rudi picked Kyle.

I picked Cates.

Rudi picked his brother Ricki.

I picked Alice.

Rudi picked Joey Angelo.

Mistake. Joey was good, but he should have
picked a catcher. I picked Ryan Feldman. Rudi
grimaced as he realized his mistake. He had
to pick Tubby next because he knew if I picked
Tubby next, he'd have no catcher at all. Of course
I wouldn't have picked Tubby next, because it
was only a practice and it wouldn't be fair for
our team to have both catchers.

Anyway, I picked Tommy Benson next.

Rudi picked Kevin Gross.

I picked Brian Seitz. We were both into subs now.

Rudi picked Calvin Hucker.

I picked Stan DiMasso.

Rudi picked Steven Carlson.

I picked Jeremy Cohen. And that left the bottom of the barrel: Art Castleton and Fred Hirth, who were computer experts but not ball players.

Rudi picked Hirth and I got stuck with Castleton.

"All right," Grampa said, "since Rudi picked first, Andy gets his choice of home team or visitors.

"Home team," I said.

"The Rudis bat first," Grampa announced, "the Andys are in the field. Coach, unless you've got a chest protector and mask, I suggest you ump from behind the pitcher. I'll be third base coach for both teams. All right, captains"—Grampa looked at his watch—"you've got exactly two minutes to set your lineups."

"Over here," I shouted.

"Over here," Rudi shouted.

Two huddles were formed.

"This is neat," Alice said in our huddle.

"Quiet," I ordered. "He said two minutes, he means two minutes."

"You just wasted ten seconds," Wally said.

I ignored him. "Alice, you're playing short. Cates, you're at first. Tommy at third. Ryan, you're catching. Go get your gear on. Brian, you play second. Don't mess up."

"I will," Brian Seitz said.

"If you say you will, then you will."

"Five seconds wasted," Castleton said.

I gave him a dirty look. "Stan, you're in center. Jeremy in left. Castleton, stay awake in right field. I'm pitching."

"Time's up," Grampa said. "Let's play ball."

"Don't we get warm-up pitches, Gram—" I stopped. "—Coach," I said, knowing it would be funny if I called Grampa "Grampa" or, worse yet, "Mr. Harris."

"Six warm-up pitches. Let's go. Let's go."

While Ryan put on his chest protector and shin guards, Grampa warmed me up. He squatted behind the plate.

I threw easy and then harder and harder . . . zipping it right in. Grampa nodded.

"Will you warm me up too, Mr. Harris?" Rudi asked.

"Darn tootin', I will." Grampa handed the catcher's glove to Ryan. "Got your signals straight?"

"No," Ryan said.

I laughed and then shouted. (It was only

an intrasquad game.) "One's a fastball. Two's a curve. Three's a change-up. Four's a split-finger."

Everyone laughed except Grampa, who said, "Let's cut the comedy. Team at bat, over here."

He huddled with the team at bat. He had to be giving them his third base coaching signals. I called Ryan out to the mound. "Look, give any signals you want," I said. "I'll shake off some but don't pay attention. They'll all be fastballs."

There was clapping from the sidelines.

Mrs. Gomez yelled: "Go Rudis."

Mrs. Feldman yelled: "Go Andys."

You'd have thought we were playing for the championship.

Their huddle broke up. Grampa trotted to the third base coaching box.

"All set, Ump?" Grampa asked Mr. Cartwright, who was standing behind me.

"Yes, sir," Mr. Cartwright said.

"Batter up then!" Grampa yelled from the third base coaching box. He had just taken over the ump's job too. Poor Mr. Cartwright. I had to laugh.

Kyle stepped in. Their team shouted. So did mine. And then began a baseball game I would never forget. Though I've tried to a thousand times.

18

I threw a pitch high for a ball and then a high hard one for a strike. Kyle was fast and liked to bunt his way on, and it's tough to bunt a high fast one.

My third pitch was low. Sure enough, Kyle squared around and bunted but it came right back at me. I whipped it sidearm to Wally and Kyle was out by four steps.

"Time, Ump," Grampa said. "Get me a bat, son," he said to Jeffrey. "You . . ." he said, pointing to Kyle, who was trotting back to the bench. "C'mere."

Jeffrey proudly delivered a bat to Grampa, looking out of the corner of his eye to make sure his second-grade buddies were watching.

"Son, you were squared around for a sacrifice. That's no way to bunt yourself on base. Andy, throw a ball."

I'd never pitched to Grampa in a gamelike

situation. Should I throw easy or hard? No, it's only practice. I threw easy down the middle.

Grampa didn't square around to bunt. He looked as though he was going to swing, and then at the very last second, his right hand slid up the barrel of the bat and he made contact with the ball and was off and running . . . all in the same motion.

The ball died in the grass ten feet down the third base line. Grampa was halfway to first.

Someone on the sidelines clapped.

Someone else yelled, "Sign that guy up."

"He looks older than eleven," a mother said.

Everyone laughed. Grampa was breathing in and out hard as he walked back to the plate.

I ran over. "Grampa, are you OK?"

"I'm fine, boy." And then to prove it, he spat. Another major league spit.

"You get the idea, son?" he said to Kyle. "There's buntin' to move a man along. And there's buntin' to get on."

He took another breath. "OK, let's get the next batter in there." He walked slowly back to the third base coaching box.

"Is your grampa OK?" Mr. Cartwright asked me quietly.

I wanted to say "no" but I didn't think Grampa would like that, so I said "yep" and wished Wally's dad would show up.

Maybe the best way to stop Grampa from demonstrating stuff was to strike out everyone fast. I'd give it a try.

Joey Angelo was up next. He was a starter, our regular second baseman, and a good contact hitter. Hard to strike out because he didn't take a big swing.

I burned three straight pitches in for strikes. Joey never took his bat off his shoulder.

After the second pitch, Grampa shouted down at Joey to choke up. Joey did but he never swung.

"He's not gonna walk you, son, and you can't get your bat around against that kind of smoke unless you choke up."

I got goose bumps hearing Grampa refer to my pitching as "smoke."

Batting third was Ricki Gomez, Rudi's twin brother. Ricki bats lefty. You can always tell them apart at the plate.

I motioned for Stan DiMasso in left to move closer to the foul line. I'd be throwing nothing but fastballs and I didn't believe Ricki could get around on them.

He didn't. He popped up to Alice at short. We trotted in and some parents cheered. I heard one mother say it was already a better season than last year.

"What's the batting order, Andy?" Brian Seitz asked.

"Tommy bats first. Alice, you're hitting second. Ryan, you're three. Wally, clean up."

"Why not you clean up?" Wally Cates asked.

"I'm gonna bat where the pitcher bats in a major league game. Last."

"You trying to give us a little class, Andy?" Ryan asked, grinning.

"Whatever works," I said. "Besides, it's only a three-inning game and we may need some power at the end."

I batted Seitz fifth. DiMasso six. Jerry Cohen seven. Castleton eight and I batted ninth.

"Listen up, Andys," Grampa said, coming into our huddle after warming up Rudi a little. "There'll be only two signals comin' down from your third base coach. And don't worry about the Rudis stealin' 'em. They've got different ones. If I touch both my shoulders . . . it's take. Touch shoulder elbow shoulder, it's hit away. You steal on your own. If I want you to bunt I'll yell 'be a banger in there.' The banger stands for bunt. I'll change that signal every inning. Who's up first?"

"I am, sir," Tommy Benson said.

"Make him throw a strike before you start swingin'. Batter up!"

Rudi finished his warm-up tosses with Tubby. He didn't throw as hard as I did but he was crafty. He could nip corners.

Tommy took the first pitch right down the middle for a strike. I was sure then that Grampa had given them the same instructions. Make the pitcher throw a strike first. Well, Rudi was no dummy.

Grampa yelled down to Tommy to "bang away" and I realized Grampa was testing us. He'd just shown us how to bunt our way on.

Rudi wound up and threw, and Tommy bunted and ran just the way Grampa had demonstrated. It was a good bunt but Rudi was quick off the mound. Which was a good thing, since Tubby, his catcher, hadn't moved at all.

Rudi threw out Tommy by a step.

"Except for the catcher not gettin' off the dime, that was a good play all around. Good bunt. Good field. Good stretch at first. Coach, I think you got a ball club on your hands."

Mr. Cartwright smiled. I think he knew what everyone was thinking. If we had the makings of a good ball club this year, it was no thanks to him.

"Your grampa's great, Andy," Brian Seitz whispered to me. "Is he gonna be here all summer?"

"He might." I yelled to Alice, "Little bingle, Alice. Rudi can't pitch. C'mon, guys, talk it up for Alice."

Our bench started yelling at once.

"Bang one out, Alice."

"Gomez can't pitch."

"Give it a ride, Cartwright."

And Rudi's team started hollering too.

"Blow it by her, Rudi."

"No stick up there."

"She's lookin' for a walk."

Watson Chevrolet had never talked it up in the field before. We'd never talked it up on the bench either.

Blowing a big pink bubble, Alice stepped in. She swung with a choked bat. The way Grampa showed her. She took a pitch and then hit a hard grounder to Ricki Gomez at short.

"Run," we yelled. Everyone was up and yelling.

Ricki threw her out by a step. But when she came back to the bench, we high-fived with her as though she'd hit a home run.

Ryan popped up at home plate. Rudi came rushing in and waved off Tubby, who looked pretty happy to be waved off. Rudi caught it for the third out. Three up, three down for both sides.

In a three-inning game, you're apt to have a pitchers' battle. Each pitcher throwing hard, knowing he's only gonna be in there a short time.

In the top of the second, I got Rudi to line out to Alice. Hucker grounded out to Wally at first. And I struck out Tubby on three straight pitches. Though from his new sitting batting stance, he took some good level cuts.

"That's the way to swing, Tubby," Grampa said. "You'll start timin' those pitches."

Tubby looked pleased despite having struck out. Morale was definitely up.

Rudi was in a groove. In our half of the second, he struck out Cates and Feldman. And got Brian to pop out to Ricki at short.

Top of the third I struck out the side. I was coming down over my head the way Grampa had showed me yesterday. No curves. No side-arm. No fooling around. Just straight fastballs. Even though Ryan was giving me signals and I would shake some off. I wasn't fooling anyone. I was just comin' after them.

Parents clapped after each out. It was a tight ball game. 0–0. Last year we usually lost by football scores. 14–3. 20–10. This year it was going to be different. We were finally learning how to play baseball. How to bear down, concentrate.

The little intrasquad practice game was coming to an end. We were in for our last licks. Jeremy Cohen, Art Castleton, and myself.

"Hey, Mr. Harris," Cates called out, "do we play extra innings if it's still 0–0?"

"A three-inning game's a three-inning game,

son. You don't want to leave your fire here. You're gettin' ready for your first real game tomorrow."

"That's right," someone said.

"Tomorrow'll be a breeze," someone else said.

"Will you be here tomorrow, Mr. Harris?" Rudi asked.

"Might be. You never know."

"I hope so," Tubby said.

"Batter up," Grampa said.

Our number-seven hitter was Jeremy Cohen, who was the best artist in our class. He concentrated hard and hit a ground ball down to Hucker at third. It was the first time I ever saw Jeremy hit a ball. We clapped for him.

Then poor little Art Castleton struck out swinging. Grampa told him not to worry, just to keep his head down when he swung, eye on the ball. "You'll get your share of hits, son."

And Art beamed.

"Last out," Joey Angelo called out as I came up to bat.

"Let's get this punk and go home," Tubby said.

I laughed.

"No stick in there, Rudi," Kyle yelled from center field.

"Stick it in his ear," Kevin Gross shouted from left field.

The Rudis were as pumped up as the Andys. It was wonderful.

I looked down to Grampa. He gave me the hit-away sign.

Rudi was a control pitcher. You could wait a month of Sundays for him to walk you. He'd also been getting that first pitch in there. I decided that if it was in there, I'd whale it.

"Number-nine batter," Kyle yelled.

"Pickin' peaches, Rudi."

"Easy out, man."

Rudi wound up. I watched the ball leave his hand. I could see the seams. It was fat and right down the middle. Wait. Wait. Wait. And . . . whip it!

I whipped my bat around and hit that ball as solidly as I'd ever hit a baseball in my life. The ball shot over the shortstop and headed for the gap in left center.

As I ran to first, I heard everyone yelling. The din was tremendous. I rounded first and saw Kyle in center and Kevin in left chasing the ball. I really turned it on then.

I rounded second and headed for third. Kyle was picking up the ball. Ricki had gone out into short left field to receive the throw and make the relay home. Our bench was screaming: "All the way, Andy. Home run!"

Grampa was halfway down the foul line waving me home, his arm making big fast loops.

"All the way," he shouted too.

I hit the third base bag and headed for home. Oh no! Tubby was blocking the plate, reaching for a catch, stretched out like a first baseman.

"Get out of the way, Tubby," I yelled.

The ball was bouncing in the dirt in front of him. It bounced into his mitt. He didn't know he had it. He was off balance, looking for the ball. All I had to do was hit him. He and the ball would be separated.

It was legal too. The base path belonged to the runner. Grampa had said that.

What I'm taking so long to describe actually happened in a split second. Tubby looked up and saw me bearing down on him like a runaway truck. He froze. Fear and panic in his eyes.

I couldn't hit him. I hit the brakes. I stopped. And Tubby sort of fell into me. I held him up or he would have fallen down.

"Out," Mr. Cartwright said quietly.

Tubby and I stared at each other. Everyone else was staring at us too. Players, spectators, parents, second graders . . . Silence was everywhere. And then Grampa's voice cut through it.

"That was the worst piece of base runnin' I ever saw in my life," he said. He turned to our

184

bench. "What do you do when the catcher's blockin' the plate?"

"You hit him," my teammates said.

"That's right. You hit him."

"Are you all right, Andy?" Mr. Cartwright asked quietly, looking me over.

"I'm fine," I said. But I wasn't.

Then, even though he was standing next to me, Mr. Cartwright said very loudly and clearly: "I thought what you did was wonderful, Andy. I'm proud of you."

"What he did, Coach, was garbage," Grampa snapped. "You play the game to win. There's no other reason to play."

"I don't agree, Mr. Harris," Mr. Cartwright said quietly. "There are things as important as winning, and good sportsmanship is among them. I think Andy showed that."

"He showed crap," Grampa said, and spat. A hard shot into the ground in front of him. Then he turned and looked at me. Those ball hawk-blue eyes looked right through me.

"There was no way that kid could have tagged you out, Andy. He didn't even know he had the ball. All you had to do was bang into him."

"I could've hurt him, Grampa."

"Hogwash. You would've knocked the air out of him for five minutes."

"Tubby's my friend, Grampa. It's—"

185

"You don't have friends on the other team when you're in a ball game."

"—only a practice game."

"A game's a game. Practice, exhibition, regular, playoff, World Series. A game's something you play to win. There's no other point in playin'. I could never get that through to your father. But he wasn't an athlete. And you are. Your not competin' is a sin. You were the winnin' run and you quit. You quit on me."

The blood was pounding in my head with every word he said. I wanted to wake up from this bad dream. I turned away from Grampa. The three second graders were staring at us. Mr. Cartwright was trying to move Watson Chevrolet out of earshot, over to the first base side bench.

But Grampa wasn't through with me. His voice was hoarse. He spat. It was another major league shot.

"Listen to me, Andy. It's okay to be soft off the field but not on the field. On the field you've got to be tough. Otherwise, all you'll end up doin' is collectin' paper heroes like he did."

And then he cleared his throat to spit again. I didn't stick around to see if it was gonna be a major league or minor league spit. I started running. In my baseball shoes. I grabbed my glove and sneakers off the bench. As I ran by my team, Mr. Cartwright called out to me: "Andy, we're having a team meeting now. Could you come here, please?"

I ran past Kyle's mother and the other parents who were folding up lawn chairs.

The guys on our team and Alice yelled after me, but I kept on running.

When I reached the corner of Granger and Baldwin, I thought I heard Grampa's voice calling my name.

But I didn't stop. If that's what it took to be Ace 459, I didn't want any part of it. Or him.

19

At the corner of Granger and Baldwin I could have gone left and been home in two seconds, but Grampa would be there in two minutes and I didn't want to ever see him again. I turned right and ran down Granger.

I didn't know where I was going. I only knew that I wanted to put as much distance between him and me as possible.

Glove in one hand, sneakers in the other, I ran west down Granger. I was wrecking my baseball shoes running on a sidewalk, but that was all right with me. I was through with baseball anyway.

At the corner of Packard and Granger, at the stop light, I looked back to see if he was coming after me. He wasn't. I didn't have to run hard anymore.

When the light turned green, I crossed Packard and ran, more slowly now, down Granger to where it dead-ended in State Street. I had to wait awhile there for traffic to clear. Overhead a blue-and-red helicopter clattered. There were a lot of trucks. I heard the wail of a fire engine or ambulance behind me. Finally there was a break in the traffic. And I ran across State Street.

Then I was on Ferry Field, where there are softball games sometimes and where busses park on football Saturdays. I walked past the football stadium. And then I was on Main Street where the American Legion Hall was, and suddenly I knew where I was going.

Probably my legs had known all along. I walked up Pauline Boulevard. Until three blocks past the Seventh Street intersection, when I saw the little woods behind the subdivision.

It's funny how your legs know things before your mind does.

That other time when Dad and I had cut through two backyards to get into the woods, no one was there. This time a man was out digging up his garden.

"Lookin' for something, son?"

"Is it OK if I go into the woods?" I asked.

Grampa would probably have knocked the guy down and taken a ladder out of his garage. That's what tough guys did.

The man looked at my glove, my sneakers, and then at my baseball shoes.

"Got your climbing shoes on, huh?"

I hadn't thought of that. I nodded.

"I don't own the woods, son. There's a public cut-through on the next block, but since you've got this far, you can keep on going."

"My dad built a tree house there when he was a little kid."

"So he's the guilty party."

"Yes, sir."

"Don't hurt yourself now."

"I won't. Thanks."

Moments later I was in the woods. It felt different than I remembered it from three years ago. Darker. More trees. I couldn't remember where the tree house was.

Dad had pointed out trees. A hickory, a black walnut, a locust. We had looked at an old rotting log that had been filled with beetles. The tree had been near that log.

It would be funny if I came all this way and couldn't find the tree house or the ladder. There had been a ladder. We didn't use it because it had been old and rotten. A rung had come off in Dad's hands. We'd used an old stump to get a leg up.

Whoops. I banged into something. It was an old stump. It could be *the* old stump. I looked up. And around and up and . . . there it was. The planks of wood in the oak tree. Dad's tree house. It hadn't been disturbed.

I laid my glove and sneakers on a bush and got on the stump. Baseball shoes would give me a better grip than sneakers. Last time Dad had helped me up. Well, I'd have to do it on my own now.

I hauled myself up to the first big branch.

I breathed out. What had Dad said about climbing? Look first, concentrate, then go. Slow. Careful. You can do it.

I hear you, Dad.

Grab that branch there. Take your time. One move at a time. Get up on the branch to your right. Slow. That's it. Now the one to your left. Good. Now that one. Easy as pie. Easy as climbing stairs once you know what you're doing. One more big one. There you go, son. You're almost there. Don't rush it. Just . . . lift yourself onto the boards. Slow. Slow. Lift. Lift. Here you go . . . you . . . made it!

I hauled myself up onto the platform and lay there breathing hard.

You did it, Andy.

Thanks, Dad.

I sat up.

I could see the American Legion Hall and the stadium and Ferry Field and the east side of town where we lived.

Dad, I thought, I'm sitting where you sat after your fights with Grampa.

Grampa's great, Dad. He made a great practice for us. He was making a team out of us. But I couldn't crash into Tubby at home plate. Not in a million years.

You know what Grampa said to me, Dad? He said I was a quitter. I was the winning run. He said it was OK to be soft off the field but on the field you had to be tough.

But I'm not tough, Dad. I'm me in both places. I'm soft in both places.

Like maybe you were.

I heard Mom tell Grampa I was a lot like you, Dad, and I thought she was wrong. But she wasn't, was she? I mean, I ran to your tree house just the way you used to. I ran away from Grampa too. And I'm sitting here just the way you used to. But I'm not gonna cry, Dad, the way you used to.

I'm not gonna cry, because Grampa's wrong, Dad. He's great and he's tough and he's Ace 459 and he's wrong.

I'm not gonna cry, Dad, 'cause you cried for us both. Oh, Pop, I love you. I love you so much. I miss you so much.

And then I cried.

20

It was dark when I got home. The house was dark. Grampa's Buick was not in the driveway. I rang the bell. No one was home.

"Hey," I yelled up at the dark windows. "Anyone here?"

I heard a window open across the street.

"Is that you, Andy?" our neighbor, Mrs. O'Dell, called out.

"Yes, ma'am," I called back.

"Your mother told me to keep an eye out for you. Come over here."

I ran across the lane.

"Your mother left your house key with me. I'm too lame to go down the stairs. Can you catch it if I drop it?"

"Sure."

She dropped the key out her window. I caught it in my glove.

"Where's my mom, Mrs. O'Dell?"

"Your grampa took sick and she drove him

to the hospital. She said for you to wait at home."

My knees began to wobble.

"Now don't worry. If your grampa were really bad, they would've called for an ambulance. He walked into the car. I saw it myself. You go home now and wait for your mother."

My heart was pounding as I let myself in the house. I turned on lights. There was a note for me on the dining room table.

Andy,

I've taken Grampa to hospital. He's all right. I'll be back as soon as I can. Leftovers in fridge.

Mom

Maybe I ought to call the hospital. But which one? There were three hospitals in town. University Hospital, the Catholic hospital, the veterans' hospital.

As I was trying to decide which one to call first, the phone rang. I grabbed it.

"Mom?"

"It's me," Tubby said.

"Oh."

"I'm callin' up to say I'm glad you got your grampa's card. I'm gonna give Alice back her quarter so it's a gift from me to you."

If I hadn't been so worried, I would have

194

laughed. That whole business seemed to have taken place a long time ago.

"Also . . . you there, Andy?"

"Yeah."

"Thanks for not hitting me this afternoon."

"Forget it."

"Your grampa was really sore at you. My dad says you should've hit me too. But I don't think so. You want to look at baseball cards tomorrow before our game?"

It was Tubby's way of making up.

"I don't think so, Tubs."

"You sure?"

"Yeah."

"We still friends?"

"Yeah."

"Your grampa coming to the game tomorrow?"

"I don't think so."

Tubby was silent. "I'll see you, Andy."

"I'll see you at the game, Tubs."

I said that instinctively. So much for being finished with baseball.

The front door opened. I ran to it. It was Mom. She held out her arms and I ran into them.

"Is he OK?"

"Yes. He had a slight heart attack. But he's resting comfortably right now."

"He's gonna be all right, then."

"The doctors think so. They're pretty sure that

when he feels better he's going to have to have that bypass operation he says he doesn't need, doesn't want, and can't afford." Mom smiled as she said that.

"Was he home when . . ."

She knew what I was worrying about. She shook her head. "Kyle's mother found him leaning against the telephone pole on the corner of Granger and Ferdon. She was chasing him to get an autograph. It's funny how life works, isn't it? If she hadn't wanted that autograph, who knows what might have happened?"

"It was my fault, Mom. He and I had a fight."

"He told me all about it on the way to the hospital. He's sorry. He's very sorry. Your grandfather's a man who never completely grew up. Now you know, don't you?"

"About him and Dad?"

"Yes. About him and Daddy and you too. I tried to warn you. I tried to warn both of you."

"Grampa said some awful things, Mom. In front of everyone. The guys on the team, parents, little kids . . ."

"He told me, Andy. He's sorry. He just couldn't stop himself. He goes all out, doesn't he?"

"He sure does. He coached that way too. He ran the bases, bunted, yelled, lay on the ground to show us how to slide. He made a team out of us, Mom. Mr. Cartwright couldn't have done

it in a million years." That was true. But something else was true too. "Mr. Cartwright stood
up for me, Mom. He stood up to Grampa.
He was nice. He—" I was starting to cry all
over again. "He . . . said . . . I did the . . .
right . . . thing . . ."

Now I was crying about Mr. Cartwright. When
was it going to end? I'd had enough crying from
myself.

Mom took me in her arms. She kissed me.

"So you found out a man can know nothing
about baseball and be nice. And you found out
a man can know everything about baseball and
not be nice. Here, blow your nose." She gave
me a handkerchief, and I blew my nose and
gave her hanky back.

She watched me. "What time did you get
home?"

"A few minutes ago."

"Where did you go?"

"Over to Dad's old tree house."

She smiled. "It was also where your father
used to go when the war between him and
Grampa got too bad. He went there to lick his
wounds too. Listen, Andy, you asked me once
if Grampa loved Daddy, and I told you he did.
And it's true. He loved him a lot. He also loves
you a lot. Do you understand that?"

I didn't understand that at all but I nodded.

Mom was the last person in the world I wanted to fight with now.

"Believe me, he does. It's as hard for him to show it to you as it was for him to show it to Daddy. But he does love us, and, Andy, we're all the family he's got now. He'll be home in a few days, and he'll stay with us while he gets his strength back. After that, he's going to have that operation and then he'll stay with us until he's well enough to go back to Arcadia. It's not going to be easy for Grampa to let us help him. But we're going to. You and me."

I wasn't sure I liked the idea of Grampa staying with us. "Maybe they won't operate on him," I said. "Doctors charge a lot and he doesn't have money."

Mom laughed. "You sound just like him now. No, they'll operate and the money will get managed and you and Grampa will get along just fine. Now go upstairs and wash the ball game off your face."

She made it all sound so simple. Grampa and I would get along fine, the money would be managed, and I would wash the ball game off my face. As though it was just a ball game I'd be washing off.

I went upstairs and into my room and looked at Ace 459 up on my bulletin board. Young, raw-boned, tough. And now he was lying alone in a hospital.

I looked at Ace 459 a long time and I thought about him and Dad. And then about me, him, and Dad. Because we were all in this together now: the three of us.

I thought about that a long time, and then I went into the closet and got out Dad's cards and his printout and Mr. Kessler's letter.

I looked at the letter and at Dad's printout and I thought: I know how to end the war for all of us.

I went into the hall and dialed The Grandstand.

"Grandstand," Mr. Kessler said in his familiar old sour voice. It was reassuring to hear it again.

"Mr. Kessler, this is Andy Harris. Soon as they let me, I wanna sell all my dad's baseball cards."

There was a silence on the other end.

"Why?" Mr. Kessler asked, still sounding grumpy.

"My grampa needs money for an operation. He's in the hospital now. He's going to be all right, but he needs money."

The silence seemed to go on forever now. When Mr. Kessler finally spoke up, his voice sounded funny.

"You hold on to those cards, Andy. Your grampa's got friends who'll pay whatever his health insurance doesn't."

"You don't understand, Mr. Kessler. *Dad* and *I* want to help him."

"I see," Mr. Kessler said, though I didn't see how he could.

"Well, you come on down sometime and we'll talk about it." He paused. "By the way, were you planning to sell them all?"

I thought about that. "I guess I'll hold on to Ace 459."

More silence. And then Mr. Kessler cleared his throat and said in his old sourpuss voice, "Well, you wouldn't get more than a quarter for it, would you?"

I laughed. "No, I guess not."

After we hung up, I went back in my room and put away the cards and the printout and the letter, and looked once more at Ace 459 up on my bulletin board.

"I love you, Grampa," I said.

Then I went into the bathroom and washed the ball game off my face.